DEADLY TRUTH

A CUSP Files Novella

ANTHONY M. STRONG

WEST STREET

ALSO BY ANTHONY STRONG

THE JOHN DECKER SUPERNATURAL THRILLER SERIES

Soul Catcher (prequel) • What Vengeance Comes • Cold Sanctuary
Crimson Deep • Grendel's Labyrinth • Whitechapel Rising
Black Tide • Ghost Canyon • Cryptic Quest • Last Resort
Dark Force • A Ghost of Christmas Past • Deadly Crossing
Final Destiny

THE CUSP FILES SERIES

Deadly Truth • Devil's Forest

THE REMNANTS SERIES

The Remnants of Yesterday • The Silence of Tomorrow

STANDALONE BOOKS

The Haunting of Willow House • Crow Song

AS A.M. STRONG WITH SONYA SARGENT

PATTERSON BLAKE FBI MYSTERY SERIES

Never Lie To Me • Sister Where Are You • Is She Really Gone
All The Dead Girls • Never Let Her Go • Dark Road From Sunset

DEADLY TRUTH

West Street Publishing

This is a work of fiction. Characters, names, places, and events are products of the author's imagination. Any similarity to events or places, or real persons, living or dead, is purely coincidental.

Copyright © 2023 by Anthony M. Strong
All rights reserved.

No part of this book may be reproduced in any form or by any electronic or mechanical means, including information storage and retrieval systems, without written permission from the author, except for the use of brief quotations in a book review.

Cover art and interior design by Bad Dog Media, LLC.

ISBN: 978-1-942207-47-4

1

ON A COLD NOVEMBER evening in the small town of Blatchford, Pennsylvania, all hell broke loose, for a little while at least.

It began with Maria Brock, a mousy forty-four-year-old woman who found herself pregnant at seventeen, married to the man who got her pregnant at eighteen, and had spent the last six months wondering if that man was cheating on her.

She said nothing, of course. She didn't even look for concrete proof of his philandering because that would mean she must do something about it. The last thing she wanted was a confrontation because truth be told, Maria was scared. She had spent her entire adult life with Marvin and wasn't sure she would know what to do without him. Worse, she probably wouldn't be able to survive. Sure, she'd recently taken a job at the local Dime Mart convenience store working the afternoon shift five days a week. But the pay was lousy, and it certainly wouldn't cover the bills. For that, she needed Marvin's paycheck. So, she swallowed her pride and looked the other way, while her husband had his fun.

At least until tonight.

She didn't start the evening intending to confront her husband. When he called and said the plant wanted him to work late, for the third time that week, she said okay. She told him dinner would be waiting when he came home, and that she would probably get an early night. And when she said those things, she meant them. She made her own dinner and put her husband's meal in the fridge to reheat when he came in. He would be hungry. He was always hungry after he worked late, even though she knew full well that there was a freeze on overtime and that Frank Peters, who lived next door and worked the same shift, always came home on time.

That done, Maria made her way to the living room and turned on the TV. Her favorite show was on. The one where couples in better relationships than hers searched for holiday homes in sunny climes. She often daydreamed that she was the one on the television, picking between three fantastic properties, while her partner—not Marvin of course because she couldn't imagine him anywhere tropical—agreed that they needed double vanities, a chef's kitchen, and a view of the ocean from their master suite.

She settled down to watch the show with a tall glass of iced tea and a king-size Hershey's bar—there was only one brand of chocolate a proud Pennsylvanian could eat—and tried to distract herself from thinking about what her husband was doing at that very moment. And at first it worked, just like it always did. The couple in the show followed their much too attractive realtor from property to property, pointing at the things they liked, and also the things they didn't like, which were mostly superficial crap that most normal people wouldn't care about. But then, as the young couple with too much money arrived at their third and final property, something happened.

She decided she would not put up with it a moment longer. If she was honest with herself, she hated sitting at home while he screwed around. She didn't want to pretend anymore.

Maria stood up. The Hershey bar fell from her lap onto the floor, but she didn't notice. Instead, she paid a brief visit to the kitchen, then returned a moment later and crossed to the hallway closet to fetch her coat. It wouldn't be hard to find Marvin. She had long suspected who he was fooling around with. It was that blonde tramp Melanie Baker who worked in the front office at the plant. The one he couldn't stop talking about because he was too stupid to realize he was giving the game away. Either that or he didn't care. Maybe deep down he wanted her to leave him. Their daughter, the reason she married him in the first place, was now all grown up and living in New York City. Their nest, as the phrase went, was empty.

She knew where the woman lived, too.

It wasn't hard to find out about such things these days. Everything was on the web. All it took was a little cyberstalking through social media sites and the state's online voter registration database.

Maria stepped out into the street, and without bothering to close the front door, started toward the condo apartments down near the river. The ones Melanie could afford, but they could not. When she remembered the front door, Maria almost turned back, but then decided she didn't care. The need to tell Marvin how she felt was too strong. It wasn't anger so much as a desire to be honest and finally lay it all out. Not that Maria wasn't angry, because she was. Actually, furious would be a better word. It bubbled up like water from a spring, filling the cavities of her previous reticence with a newfound resolve.

But she never made it to the tramp's condo, because halfway there she spotted Marvin coming up the street toward her, walking like he had somewhere to be. Striding along with more confidence than she would previously have given him credit for. And when he spotted Maria, he didn't even slow down. He just approached and didn't stop until they were face-to-face.

"I need to be honest with you," he said, breathless. "I'm seeing someone else. It's Melanie from work."

Maria said nothing. This stark and unexpected admission by her husband crystalized within her the reality of her true feelings. She didn't want an honest chat with Marvin. Didn't want to work things out. She loathed him. She had been lying to herself for too long, making excuses that she needed him, hiding behind a ridiculous fear of being alone.

But not anymore.

Maria was going to face the truth of her feelings head on. And the cold hard truth was that she wanted Marvin to die. Which was why she didn't hesitate to raise the kitchen knife —the one she'd used to prepare his dinner and couldn't actually remember bringing outside—and plunge it into his chest before he could even react.

While behind her in the street, twenty-six-year-old Megan Schultz, who worked with Maria at the Dime Mart, was busy smashing her boyfriend's souped-up Mustang with a baseball bat, because she finally accepted the reality that he would never look at her the way he looked at his beloved car.

Further away, an elderly man in slippers and a robe chased his wife down the sidewalk to tell her, after fifty years, how much he hated the way she cooked Brussels sprouts.

And in the distance police sirens wailed, responding to more disturbance calls than the town of Blatchford had ever before received in a single night.

2

Colum O'Shea, former Irish Army Ranger Wing Special Forces soldier, and now an operative for the shadowy organization known as Classified Universal Special Projects, referred to as CUSP, tore open the manila envelope his employer had given him and deposited the items contained within upon the table.

It was late. Past midnight.

Colum was the lone occupant of a motel room near the highway outside of Blatchford, Pennsylvania, to which he had driven from his employer's secluded island headquarters off the coast of Maine. He was, until a week ago, assigned to the Irish field office out of Dublin. Not anymore. His skills were needed stateside, and so here he was, at least for the foreseeable future.

Colum spread the contents of the envelope out and studied them. A driver's license, several credit cards, and an FBI shield attached to a black leather credential wallet. He picked up the wallet and opened it, wondering who he was going to be for the next few days, or maybe longer.

Special Agent Dale Winters.

Do I look like a Dale? He thought to himself, studying the photograph on the credentials. He looked at least a couple of years younger than his true age of thirty-six. Thick, dark short-cropped hair, piercing green eyes, a prominent jaw line, and a muscular military physique. No, he thought to himself, he definitely didn't look like a Dale.

He examined the rest of the items. The license and credit cards all bore the same name as the FBI credentials. There was even a dry-cleaning garment ticket and a couple of credit card receipts that matched his alias. These were fake, of course, just like everything else, but they added realism to his cover. Best of all, if anyone checked with the Bureau, his credentials would hold up—long enough to complete the mission, at least. Such was the influence of his employer.

Colum gathered the credit cards and license and inserted them into an empty wallet purchased for this purpose. He'd stashed his real wallet containing the documentation of his true identity inside a secure locker back in Maine. Until he returned to collect it, he was Dale Winters. He had barely finished this task when there was a light knock on the hotel room door.

Colum stood and went to the door, leaving the wallet and credentials on the desk. He did, however, scoop up the Glock 19mm handgun provided to him for the duration of his stint as Special Agent Winters. He wasn't expecting trouble, but Colum had learned never to take his safety for granted. This had gotten him out of more than one situation, and would do so again, he was sure.

"Can I help you?" Colum asked, standing to the right of the closed door close to the window.

"It's me, Shelby," a female voice said. "Let me in."

Colum unlocked the door and stood back, keeping the gun half raised. "It's open."

The door swung inward. An attractive woman in her early thirties stepped through. She was slender, with shoulder length black hair and deep brown eyes. He noticed a slight bulge under her jacket. A shoulder holster, no doubt containing a Glock identical to his own. She carried a large travel bag over one shoulder.

"How was the drive?" Colum asked. He lowered the gun and turned back to the desk.

"Frustrating. A tractor-trailer jackknifed on Ninety-Five outside Richmond. Took hours to get past it." Shelby set her bag on the floor. "Then traffic was backed up through DC."

"Don't worry about it. I only got in a short while ago, myself." Colum said, sitting back down.

Shelby perched on the edge of the bed and kicked her shoes off with obvious relief. "You open your packet yet?"

"Yeah. Just did it."

"Who are you supposed to be?"

"Dale Winters. Stupid name, if you ask me. Not very imaginative."

"Not action hero enough for you?" Shelby smiled.

"Something like that." Colum had only worked with Shelby once before, on an assignment in Prague, but he liked her. She was the real deal. An actual FBI special agent recruited out of the Bureau to work for CUSP. And since they were playing feds for this gig, her past employment would add an air of authenticity, which was probably why CUSP selected her to be his partner. "What's your cover?"

"Special Agent Emily North," Shelby replied. "I like it, although they used a horrible photo on the driver's license. Makes me look chubby."

"Yeah. At least you don't have to tell everyone your name is Dale."

"Suck it up. I've heard worse cover names." Shelby grinned. "Seriously though, I'm surprised they paired us together."

"Why?" Colum raised an eyebrow. "You don't like me?"

"No. Not that." Shelby's face flushed, just a little. "I like you well enough."

"Then what?"

"Um . . . The accent?" Shelby replied. "You don't think it's odd for an FBI agent to sound so . . ."

"Irish?"

"Yes."

"I won't sound Irish when I'm being Dale Winters," Colum said. When he next spoke, his accent had morphed to American Mid-West. "I'll be playing the part, don't ya know."

"Wow." Shelby's eyes widened. "How did you do that so well?"

Colum laughed, reverting to his own accent. "My father was from Dublin, but my mother was born in Chicago. Moved to Ireland after she met my dad and still lives there. She never lost her accent, and I used to copy it as a kid. Now it comes as natural as putting on a fresh pair of socks. I don't use it much though. The girls think Irish is cuter."

"That's shallow." Shelby replied.

"Fine." Colum fell back into Mid-West. "I'll talk like this from now on, then."

"Please don't," Shelby said. "Not in private, at least."

"See," Colum said, slipping back again. "Irish is better."

"Maybe a little," Shelby agreed. "If your mother is American, does that mean you are, too?"

"Dual nationality. I have two passports."

"Must be nice." Shelby said. She covered her mouth and yawned.

"It has advantages," Colum said. "Not that it matters much. CUSP can provide whatever documents I need to go anywhere they want me."

"Right." Shelby nodded. "On that note, what time do you want to start in the morning?"

"Early. Let's meet at seven. I'd like to get over to the Sheriff's office first thing after breakfast."

"Ouch. That is early. It's almost one in the morning already. I'd better hit the sack." Shelby slipped her shoes back on and stood up. "You got my room key?"

Colum picked up a key card from the desk and handed it to her. "You're in twenty-six, next door."

"Great." Shelby took the key and picked up her bag.

Colum nodded toward an interior door next to the TV stand. "Rooms connect. My side is unlocked. You should do the same."

"You expecting trouble?" Shelby asked.

"No. Just a precaution." Colum stood and walked her to the door. "Sleep tight."

"You too." Shelby stepped out into the night and turned toward her room.

Colum waited until she was inside, then retreated to the bed and undressed. He heard the connecting door's deadbolt disengage on her side, and a voice drifted through.

"All done," Shelby called out from her room. "See you in the morning . . . Dale."

"Funny," Colum replied. "Go to sleep, that's an order."

"You're not my boss," came the reply, then there was silence.

He placed the Glock on the nightstand and prepared for bed. Then he slipped under the covers, wearing only a pair of boxers, and turned off the light. He was asleep in less than a minute.

3

When Colum left his hotel room the next morning, Shelby was waiting, leaning against the black Chevy Tahoe assigned to him by the CUSP motor pool.

"Sweet ride," she said as he crossed the parking lot. "They made me drive my POV up here. Told me to expense the gas."

"POV?" Colum asked, bewildered.

"Personally owned vehicle. It's fed-speak. Sometimes I forget I'm not in the FBI anymore."

"Ah." Colum nodded. "CUSP is about as far from the FBI as you can get."

"Tell me about it." Shelby waited for Colum to unlock the car, then jumped into the passenger seat. "Even when I was with the Bureau, I never got a ride this fancy. My first year out of Quantico, they gave me a Pontiac Firebird confiscated from a pimp in Miami. It was ten years old and ran like crap. Engine was so loud a perp could hear me coming from three blocks away."

"Nice."

"Yeah. I was so skeeved out driving it, I nagged them for a

new set of wheels for months, even though I was just a newbie. God alone knows what had gone on in that car." Shelby buckled her seatbelt. "You eat yet this morning?"

"Nope." Colum shook his head. "I figure we'll pick up a bite on the way over to the Sheriff's Office."

"And coffee."

"Goes without saying." Colum steered through the parking lot and turned onto the road. Two blocks north was a McDonalds. He pulled into the drive thru. "This okay with you?"

"It will have to be," Shelby replied. "Doesn't look like there's much else between here and town."

"Not unless you want a gas station hotdog."

"Yuck. Mickey-D's it is."

There was only one car ahead of them. When it moved, Colum pulled up to the box and ordered two Egg McMuffin meals. They ate in the car, with the takeout bag sitting on the dash. When they were done, Colum drove around to a trash can near the door, then pulled back out onto the road.

"What's your take on the situation here?" he asked, keeping his gaze rooted firmly ahead.

"Wish I knew," Shelby replied. "Eighteen domestic disturbances in one night? Five assaults. One person charged with property damage for smashing up their boyfriend's car."

"And a cold-blooded murder," Colum added. "All within a thirty-minute window."

"In a town of eight thousand. Stretches credibility."

"It's not the first such spate of condensed violence either. Happened a few weeks earlier too, although there were no serious injuries during that occurrence, thank the Lord."

"Do you have a working theory?"

"Not yet." Colum shook his head. "I want to see what local law enforcement makes of it. You?"

Shelby shrugged. "Mass hysteria?"

"Why?" Colum glanced her way. "It's not like there was any inciting event or circumstance. It was just a random and unremarkable Wednesday evening."

"There must have been a trigger. It's too many concurrent events to be coincidence."

"But what could it be?" Colum asked. "I don't see a connection between any of the disturbances. They were all in the same geographic area, to be sure, but other than that there is simply no obvious common denominator."

"Beats me," Shelby replied. "I guess we'll have to do some good old-fashioned sleuthing."

"And no better time to start than now," Colum said as they entered downtown and approached the Sheriff's Office. He pulled up at the curb outside the building in a spot marked OFFICIAL VEHICLES ONLY and opened his door.

"Wait," Shelby said. "Can we park here? I don't want to get towed."

"We're in an official vehicle. Federal plates, remember? Although don't ask me how CUSP got access to them because I don't know. Nobody will touch us."

"I hope you're right." Shelby didn't look convinced. "It's a long walk back to the hotel."

"Stop worrying. As far as anyone is concerned, we're bona fide FBI agents."

"I used to be a genuine FBI agent. That *is* why I'm worried. Do you know how much trouble we'll be in if we get caught impersonating law enforcement officers?"

"No, because it's never happened to me, and I've pretended to be everything from a British detective inspector to a CIA operative. One time I even had to go undercover as a priest, but that's a story for another day."

"A priest, huh?" Shelby suppressed a smirk.

"Yup. If only my Irish grandmother could have seen it she would have been so proud."

"Until she found out you were a fraud."

"Then she would have told me I'm going to hell." Colum started toward the entrance. "Come on, we have a sheriff to meet."

4

The Denton County Sheriff's Office and Jail sat a block off Main Street at the edge of Blatchford's crumbling downtown. It was a red brick building with a dull façade and windows that looked like no one had cleaned them in a decade. A newer structure, the jail itself, occupied a tract of land at the rear. It rose fifteen feet above the sheriff's office. An access road with a sturdy metal gate to the left of the office ran to the sallyport, where prisoners entered the jail.

Colum and Shelby hurried up the front steps and entered, crossing the small lobby and flashing their badges at the receptionist, an older woman with smoker's lines ringing her rouged lips and unruly silver locks. She picked up a phone, spoke into it for a few moments, and then buzzed them through a secure door to the left of the reception desk.

Sheriff Bartlett T. Clay was a portly man in his late fifties with a buzz cut to hide his thinning hair and rosacea that turned his cheeks ruby-red. He occupied a ten-by-ten office at the back of a communal area furnished with desks for the deputies, and doors leading off to the evidence locker, file room, and interview suites.

When Colum and Shelby entered, he pushed his chair back and rose to greet them with a grunt. "You must be the federal stiffs."

"Special Agents Dale Winters and Emily North," Colum said, easily slipping into his American accent.

"I have to say, it came as a surprise when I got the notification that you people were on the way."

"Why is that?" Colum asked.

"A few minor unrelated incidents?" Clay shrugged. "A vandalized car. Domestic disturbances. Hardly seems like the kind of thing federal law enforcement need bother itself with."

"And a murder," Shelby reminded him. "Maria Brock?"

"She killed her husband with a kitchen knife," Colum said. "Stabbed him twelve times in the chest."

"Like I said, a domestic," Clay replied. "He was cheating on her. Had been for years. She finally snapped. Wouldn't be the first time a jealous wife meted out some biblical justice."

"Except it happened on the same night as all the other disturbances. Too many in a short timeframe to be pure coincidence," Colum said.

Shelby glanced his way. "And it wasn't the only such spate, either."

"Right."

"I still don't see the need for FBI involvement. There's no federal aspect to this. No crossing of state lines. Cut and dried marital dispute." Clay folded his arms, which had the effect of highlighting his paunch and making him look even more overweight. "But hey, if the feds want to fish in my pond, who am I to say no? My budget to run this department shrinks every year so as long as I'm not footing the bill for your paychecks, I say have at it. Frees up my deputies for the real work."

"That's very magnanimous of you," Colum commented.

"Don't mention it." Clay waved a hand in the air. "You'll need to find your own place to work, too. I don't have any available desks around here."

"That's fine."

"Unless your people want to fund some new furniture? Then I'm sure I could find a little floor space." Clay looked hopeful. "Just so you can work in comfort."

"That won't be happening," Colum replied. "We can do our work from the hotel."

"Prefer it, actually," Shelby chimed in.

"Oh." The sheriff didn't bother hiding his disappointment. "That's a shame. Anyway, offer stands."

"We'll keep that in mind," Colum said. He glanced back through the open door. "Now, if we're done with the introductions, we'd like to have a chat with Maria Brock."

5

The interview room at the Denton County jail was a sparse white box that contained nothing but a metal desk and three chairs. Two of these were freestanding. The third, bolted to the floor, was made of metal. Upon this, hands cuffed behind her back, sat the person Colum and Shelby had come to see.

Maria Brock.

She was a diminutive middle-aged woman with dull flat hair that fell from her scalp like a wilted plant. Her complexion was sallow. Dark circles ringed her eyes, the skin underneath puffy and bloated. She did not look up when they entered, keeping her gaze trained on the tabletop in front of her.

Colum approached the table, with Shelby right behind, and took a seat. He sat with folded arms and observed the prisoner for a few moments before speaking. "Maria?"

She lifted her head, dusty green eyes finding his for a moment, before her gaze fell downward once more. "Yes?"

"My name is Dale Winters," Colum said in his American accent. "This here is my partner, Special Agent Emily North."

"So?"

"We'd like to ask a few questions, if you don't mind."

"I've already confessed to killing my husband. I don't know why anyone would want to talk to me again."

"Because we need to understand why you did it," Shelby said.

"I told the police that already, too." Maria's voice was lifeless, lacking emotion. "He was running around on me."

"Which he'd been doing for many years, according to the police report," Shelby said. "It wasn't a secret. Most of your friends knew what was going on, even if you wouldn't talk about it."

"Why should I talk about it? It was no one else's business."

"No, it wasn't." Shelby leaned forward with her elbows on the table. "But you knew about your husband's activities for a long time. Why choose that moment to confront him?"

Maria shrugged.

"Why do it in the street?"

Again, Maria shrugged.

"And why kill him?"

Now Maria spoke. She lifted her head and met Shelby's gaze. "The idea just came over me. I guess I didn't want to deceive myself anymore."

"Because you finally realized that ignoring his philandering wouldn't achieve anything?" Shelby asked.

"No." Maria shook her head. "Because I finally realized that I wanted him to die. I felt like, for the first time, I was being honest with myself."

"You could have just divorced him," Colum said, chipping in after letting Shelby carry the interrogation up to that point.

"And what would that have achieved? Marvin was the

breadwinner. He owned half the house. He would've just taken the money and went to live with his tramp. How would that be fair?"

"It might not be," Colum said. "But it's better than spending your life in prison. It's better than being a murderer."

"Look, I won't pretend that I hadn't fantasized about killing him before. It was embarrassing. Like you said, everyone knew what he was doing. I ignored it. Pretended I didn't know. I felt ashamed. Weak because I was too afraid to do anything about it. But I didn't start that night intending to commit a murder. Like I said, I'm weak."

"What changed?" Shelby asked.

"I don't know. I was all set to distract myself, as usual. Pretend everything was fine and dandy. I got a bar of chocolate from the pantry, went into the living room to watch TV. One of those shows where they go to exotic places and look at houses. I like to imagine that I'm one of those people, with a happy home life and the money to live somewhere sunny. It's stupid, I know." Maria paused and wiped a tear from her cheek.

"No. It's not stupid. Not at all." Colum's voice was soothing. Despite what she'd done, he felt sorry for this woman. "Do you want to continue?"

"Sure." Maria sniffed and made a visible effort to pull herself together. She flexed her arms and winced. "I wish these handcuffs weren't so tight."

"I can't do anything about that," Colum told her. "But the quicker we get this interview over, the sooner you can go back to your cell and have them removed."

"I'm going to prison for a long time, aren't I?" There was a tremble in Maria's voice.

"It would appear that way."

"That's what I thought. I wish I could go back to that evening. Don't get me wrong, I don't regret killing him. He deserved it for all he put me through. But maybe I would do things differently, for my own sake."

"It's a shame you didn't have the foresight to realize that at the time," Shelby said.

"I'm not sure foresight had anything to do with it. I wasn't consciously plotting to kill him. It was more like a revelation. Like I suddenly knew why I wasn't happy, and it was because I'd been lying to myself. I wanted to be truthful, just once. And the truth told me to kill him. It came to me in the middle of the show while the happy TV couple were looking at their second property. It was like a light being turned on. One minute I was distracting myself, trying not to imagine what he was up to at that very moment, and the next I was on my way out the door to confront him."

"To kill him, you mean," Colum said.

"Yes. I suppose that is what I mean. I don't remember taking the kitchen knife. Truthfully, the whole thing is hazy, almost like a dream. But I do remember how I felt. The thought of acting out the fantasy I'd denied myself for so long and killing my husband overcame me. It filled my entire head. It didn't even occur to me that there would be consequences. I even stood in the middle of the street and waited for the police to arrive, still holding the knife. Because it just made so much sense. It was only later that night when I was in the holding cell I realized what I'd done."

Colum and Shelby exchanged glances.

"Tell me one last thing," Colum said. "And then you can go back to your cell and get those handcuffs removed."

"Okay," Maria said.

"In your opinion, were you in full control of your actions at the moment you killed your husband, Mrs. Brock? Were you still in the driver's seat, so to speak?"

"No." Maria answered. "I would say that something else had taken control of me. At least temporarily."

"And why do you believe that?" Shelby asked.

"Because I don't think I have it in me to kill someone." Maria's head dropped again. She stared into her lap. "Because I'm not a murderer."

6

"Do you think she's going for an insanity defense?" Shelby said as they exited the sheriff's office and walked toward their car. "Voices made me do it, and all that malarkey."

"Actually, I don't." Colum replied, back to his Irish accent now they were alone. "If the murder was an isolated incident, I might be inclined to say yes, but it was just the most serious among a slew of crimes and misdemeanors that night. It's like the town collectively lost its marbles."

"Which brings us back to temporary insanity." Shelby waited for Colum to unlock the car and then climbed into the passenger seat. "Because the entire town didn't lose their marbles. Only some residents did, which could be interpreted as coincidence."

"But it's not." Colum started the engine.

"You can't be sure of that."

"No, I can't. But my gut is telling me something is very wrong in Blatchford," Colum said. "And don't forget, CUSP sent us here. They wouldn't do that unless they were sure this wasn't just an oddly timed spree of unusual incidents."

"You have a point." Shelby looked back toward the sheriff's office and the jail beyond. "Where do we go from here?"

"Megan Schultz."

"Who?"

"The woman who took a baseball bat to her boyfriend's car. She lived on the same street as Maria. I'd say that if there was an external influence at play, it's a fair bet it affected Megan Schultz too."

"A reasonable assumption." Shelby nodded. "Do you know where she is now?"

"At the time of the incident she was living with her boyfriend. She ended up arrested for criminal mischief, but her boyfriend refused to press charges and she was released the next morning."

"Well, at least we know where she isn't," Shelby said, glancing back toward the jail.

"I assume she went back to their shared accommodation," Colum said, "since the boyfriend went out of his way to get her out of trouble."

"Despite the damage she'd done to his car."

"Exactly. He's more forgiving than I would've been."

"I don't believe that," Shelby said. "You act tough, but I think deep down there's a teddy bear trying to claw its way out."

"Teddy bear?" Colum grimaced. "You trying to say I'm soft?"

"Not in the least. I'm trying to say that you're compassionate."

"You know nothing about me," Colum replied. "I've done my share of morally questionable things. When you work for Special Forces it kind of goes with the territory."

"Maybe," Shelby said. "That isn't who you are now,

though. That job we worked together in Prague last year. You had a choice between the easy way and the right way. You chose the right way and saved lives."

"I did what was necessary, Nothing more."

"Geez, I'm just trying to pay you a compliment."

"Can we get back to business?" Colum sounded uncomfortable.

"Fine. Do you have the boyfriend's address?"

"I looked it up this morning before we left the hotel," Colum replied. He took out his phone and opened the notes app, then copied the address into the car's GPS. That done, he glanced toward Shelby. "You ready to dig a little deeper?"

7

MEGAN SCHULTZ LIVED in a boxy fourplex that looked like it had been built in the fifties and didn't appear to have seen a fresh coat of paint since. A gutter hung loose off one side of the building, squeaking in the breeze. The concrete steps leading up to the wraparound porch were crumbling and had sunk on one corner. There were two doors on the porch, and another two above, accessed by a set of stairs leading to a second-floor balcony over the porch. The doors were numbered, one through four.

Outside, at the curb, sat a red late model Mustang with a dented driver's side door and front wing.

"Guess we're in the right place," Colum said, glancing toward the car as he mounted the concrete steps onto the porch with Shelby right behind. He stopped at the door marked two.

"And it sounds like someone's home," Shelby said, noting the sound of a TV playing from within the condo.

"Looks that way." Colum knocked twice on the screen door and then stepped back, waiting. When there was no answer, he knocked again. Soon enough he heard a woman's voice, almost drowned out by the TV noise.

"Hold your horses. I'm coming for Pete's sake." The inner door opened, and a young woman appeared, wearing a flannel bathrobe over a white cotton shift with pale bare legs poking out beneath. She was dowdy, with flat brown hair that fell to her shoulders and dark shadows under her eyes. A half-smoked cigarette dangled between two fingers.

"Megan Schultz?" Colum asked, in his American voice.

"Who wants to know?" The woman stood behind the aluminum screen door and peered out at Colum and Shelby.

"FBI, Ma'am." Colum took out his fake credentials and flashed them at her. "I'm Special Agent Winters. My partner here is Special Agent North."

"How are you doing?" Shelby said. She smiled a wide grin at Megan.

"FBI, huh?" Megan said, apparently unimpressed by the credentials. "There a reason you're at my door?"

"Ma'am, we just want to ask you a few questions. It won't take long."

Megan paused a moment, then shrugged and unlatched the screen door. She opened it just wide enough for them to step inside. "I guess I should let you in before my neighbors see you. Folk love to gossip, and this'll keep them going for weeks."

"Thank you," Colum said as he and Shelby entered the apartment.

Colum looked around. They were standing in a living room, kitchen combo. It was small, cramped, and in desperate need of renovation, much like the exterior of the building. A worn rug had been spread over a brown linoleum floor. There were darker squares in the faded linoleum where furniture had once been placed. A TV was playing on a flimsy stand that hugged the wall near an old sofa. Across from that was a Formica laminated table and four chairs. A pack of Marlboros and a lighter lay on the table. He saw no ashtray, but there were several burn marks on the surface of the table. The smell of cigarette smoke was overwhelming. A stack of dishes were piled in the kitchen sink, being circled by a couple of buzzing flies.

"Guess you weren't expecting company," Shelby said, wrinkling her nose.

"Maid's day off," Megan replied. She picked up the TV remote and turned the volume down. "So, what can I do for the FBI?"

"Is your boyfriend here?" Colum asked, glancing toward an open door that led into a bedroom. He could see an unmade bed beyond the threshold, with clothes piled on the floor at its foot.

"Nah. At work." Megan sauntered further into the room and plunked down on the couch. She took a long drag of the cigarette and exhaled the smoke in a thin silver stream. "You want a coffee or something?"

"No. Thank you." Colum shook his head. He could see the mistrust in her eyes. He nodded toward the front door. "That your boyfriend's car out front?"

"What, the Mustang?"

"Yes."

"Sure. It's his."

"I thought you said he was at work?" Shelby said.

"He is." Megan flicked ash onto the floor and watched it land. "He works at the paper mill out on Route Eighty. His friend picked him up today. They carpool. Saves on gas. Marcus will drive tomorrow."

"I see." Colum nodded. "Those are some pretty bad dents he has there. Marcus get into an accident?"

"Yeah. With me and a baseball bat," Megan said. "Since when do the FBI give a crap about domestic disturbances?"

Colum shrugged.

"I assume that's why you're here . . . since you made a point to mention the car."

"It is," Shelby said. "Your boyfriend refused to press charges, so we're told."

"What can I say. Marcus loves me." Megan grinned. "I keep him happy, if you know what I mean."

"So why did you bash in his car?" Colum rounded the sofa and took a seat.

Shelby stayed on her feet but moved up behind him.

"Felt like it." Megan flicked ash onto the floor again, as if to emphasize her words.

"You felt like it?" Colum raised an eyebrow. "That's it?"

"Sure." Megan looked at Colum. The grin slipped away. "You ever feel like doing something, even though you know it ain't right?"

"Sometimes." Colum nodded.

"Well, there you go. I just felt like smashing his car up a bit. So that's what I did."

"I don't buy it. There must have been a reason. You just don't want to admit it." Colum said. "Had the two of you been fighting?"

"No." Megan shook her head. "Just the opposite, actually. We were snuggled up right here on the couch. All cozy and warm."

"And then you just jumped up, grabbed a baseball bat, went outside, and whaled on his car for no good reason?"

"Sounds stupid when you put it like that, but yeah."

Megan nodded. "It was like, all of a sudden, I was angry at him. Really freaking angry."

"Because you were jealous?" Shelby asked, standing with her arms folded. "According to the police report, you told the responding officers that you hated the attention he lavished on the car."

"God. I sound like a nutjob." Megan finished her cigarette and crumpled the butt between her fingers before placing it on the arm of the sofa. "Look. I don't know what happened any more than you do. Like I said, we were sitting on the sofa, then I got real angry out of nowhere. All I could think about was that car, and how he spends every weekend cleaning it, and polishing it. How he drives it to the hotrod meet at Cooley's every first Friday."

"Cooley's?" Colum asked.

"Yeah. The burger joint downtown. The car club meets there to show off their rides. Lift their hoods, drink beer, and stare at each other's engines." Megan shook her head. "I remember standing up, just full of rage. I suddenly realized that the car was my rival and while it was here he'd never love me the most. I opened the closet and took out the baseball bat. We keep it there in case of trouble. This isn't the best neighborhood."

"We noticed," Colum said. "Please, continue."

"So, I went to the door. Marcus asked where I was going but I didn't answer him. Next thing I know, I'm out on the street and pounding on that car, bringing the bat down again and again."

"Then what?" Shelby came around the sofa, finally, and stood looking at Megan.

"Marcus was screaming at me to stop. He tried to grab the bat, but I pushed him away. God, it was like I was possessed. Then, as quick as the anger came, it went. Just sort of disappeared, like a switch being turned off. That's when I realized what I'd done. I dropped the bat and ran back in the house, locked myself in the bedroom. I thought Marcus was going to kill me. The cops showed up a little while later."

"And you haven't felt that way again since?"

"No." Megan shook her head. "I can't explain it. It was sort of like I was dreaming. You know when you wake up from a nightmare? That's how it felt. Kind of weird and disjointed. I knew what I did but it was as if someone else was in my head, making me do that stuff. Pushing my buttons."

Colum exchanged a glance with Shelby then looked back to Megan. "I have one more question, if you don't mind."

"Sure." Megan nodded.

"Did you have anything to eat or drink before the incident? Like tea or coffee. A glass of water?"

"I don't remember. A coffee maybe. Why?"

"No reason," Colum said, standing and turning toward the door. "Thank you Megan. You've been most helpful."

8

BACK OUTSIDE OF Megan Schultz's house, Colum glanced at Shelby. "So, what do you think?"

"Honestly, I don't know." Shelby looked perplexed as they descended the concrete steps and made their way back to the car. "But I'm beginning to think you're right. There is outside influence at play."

"Has to be." Colum unlocked the car and climbed in, then waited for Shelby to join him before continuing. "Both women described similar experiences. They both said they didn't feel in control of themselves, as if someone else was behind the wheel."

"Like they were possessed," Shelby said.

"I don't believe in possession." Colum started the car. "Despite my Catholic upbringing."

"Neither do I."

"Then where does that leave us?" Colum pulled out and turned in the motel's direction. There were no more leads to follow in town, and he wanted to do some research, settle behind his laptop, and dig a little deeper into Blatchford.

Maybe he would find a new line of inquiry. Or maybe he wouldn't.

"Whatever affected people that night, it wasn't supernatural. That much I'm sure of. A drug in the water supply, maybe?"

"The thought crossed my mind," Colum admitted. "But the incidents were random. The entire town drinks from that water supply. Everyone should have succumbed to its effects if the water was tainted."

"Not necessarily. It might only have affected those people who had made a drink during a specific time frame. Don't forget, Maria Brock was drinking iced tea before she killed her husband."

"But Megan Schultz didn't remember whether she was drinking anything."

"But we can't rule it out. She did say she might have had a cup of coffee."

"Hardly a smoking gun."

"We have nothing else." Shelby pulled her phone out and started surfing the web. She clicked away for a few moments and then looked back at Colum. "The utility company has a water treatment plant in the next county. That's the most logical point of access for a contaminant. Especially if it's deliberate."

"I'm still not sure." Colum shook his head. "That treatment plant won't just provide water to Blatchford, and nowhere else has reported any unusual incidents. Whatever is going on, it's confined to this locale. Also, it appears to be time specific. All the incidents occurred within a very narrow window. It would be insanely difficult to control a drug in the water supply with such a high level of precision."

"More like impossible."

"Exactly. I'm not ruling the water supply out, I just think we should pursue other avenues of investigation, too." Colum's gaze shifted to the rear-view mirror and then back to the road ahead. His brow furrowed. "This might sound paranoid, but I think we have a tail. Black sedan with tinted windows. It was sitting at the curb when we left Megan's house and pulled out behind us. I've been watching and it's still there."

"What? Really?" Shelby didn't turn around. She knew better than that. It could tip their pursuers off. Instead, she leaned forward to use the passenger door mirror. "I see them, but I can't tell how many people are in the car. Are you sure they're following us?"

"One way to find out," Colum said.

He pushed down on the gas, increasing their lead from the black sedan by a few car lengths. There was an intersection with a traffic light up ahead. As Colum approached, it turned yellow. He nudged their speed a notch higher and kept going.

"Are you sure this is a good idea?" Shelby reached up and gripped the handle above her door. "I got the impression Sheriff Clay didn't like us very much and we won't win him over by driving like lunatics and running red lights in the middle of his town."

"Duly noted," Colum said. "But I want to see how that car behind us reacts. If they follow us through the intersection, then we have our answer."

"And then what? We lose them in a high-speed chase through the streets of Blatchford. Do you want to tell that to Sheriff Clay when he shows up at our door with an arrest warrant for reckless endangerment?"

"You worry too much." Colum reached the intersection.

As he zipped through, the light turned red.

The car behind them had sped up when Colum did. But now it slowed and rolled forward cautiously, coming to a halt at the light.

"Guess they weren't following us," Shelby said.

"Maybe." Colum eased off the gas pedal. He kept his eyes on the rear-view mirror. "Or maybe they worry that blowing through an intersection will draw too much attention."

"You think?" Shelby turned in her seat and risked a look behind her now.

The light turned green, and the sedan rolled forward. It sped through the intersection and closed the gap between them.

Colum had seen it too. His gaze shifted between the rear-view mirror and the road ahead. "I think we've got ourselves a problem."

"Looks that way." Shelby grimaced. "Guess I spoke too soon."

"Yeah. You have any interest in finding out who they are, and why they're tailing us?"

"What do you think?" Shelby nodded. "Let's do it."

"Glad we're on the same page." Colum activated his right turn signal and slowed, entering a side street between a convenience store and a vacant lot with a cracked concrete foundation surrounded by weeds—the building it had supported long gone.

The black sedan followed along, turning behind them but staying a suitable distance back.

"This should be interesting," Colum said, pulling over suddenly and parking up outside of what looked like a shuttered machine shop. On the other side of the road was a dive bar with a bunch of motorcycles parked up outside, mostly

Hogs. A biker stood on the pavement outside the door, talking on the phone and drinking a Budweiser. Colum killed the engine and glanced toward the bar, then turned to Shelby. "Ready to do this?"

"Hell, yes," Shelby said. "How do you want to play it?"

"We act like we haven't noticed them. Just get out of the car and act natural, as if we have business inside that bar over there. Our friends in the sedan will have no choice but to either park up and wait for us, drive past us, or turn back in the other direction." Colum opened his door. "I'm betting they'll try to slide on past as if they weren't following us. That's when we'll stop them."

"Guns drawn?"

"Well, we are the FBI." Colum grinned, then climbed out of the car.

"That's what I was afraid you'd say." Shelby climbed out and followed Colum. Together they started across the road toward the bar, keeping the black sedan in sight from the corner of their eyes.

The car was almost upon them now, but it slowed to a crawl as they passed in front of it. When the car drew within twenty feet, Colum turned to face it and reached under his jacket, removing his Glock sidearm at the same time.

Beside him, Shelby drew her own gun.

Colum saw the dark outlines of two people through the sedan's windshield.

The black car slowed further, the driver hesitating as if unsure what to do, before making up his mind.

The vehicle's engine revved.

Tires spun against asphalt with a loud squeal.

And then the sedan shot straight toward them at high speed.

9

COLUM SCRAMBLED LEFT AND DIVED. He landed hard on the asphalt, jarring his elbow, and almost lost his gun. When he sat up the car was moving fast, speeding away down the street.

Shelby had flung herself to the right, hit the ground, and rolled. They were both back on their feet seconds after the car breezed past them at high speed. Colum lifted his gun and aimed toward the receding taillights, then dropped it back to his side. The last thing he wanted was to be popping off shots on a public street.

The vehicle turned at the end of the road and disappeared from sight.

Shelby rushed over, holstering her gun as she went. "Are you okay?"

"I'll live." Colum dusted himself off and slipped his gun into its holster. "Did you get a good look at the driver?"

"No, I was too busy trying not to get killed." Shelby glanced back toward the bar, where the biker stood holding his beer. He was staring at them, wide eyed. When he saw her look his way, he dropped his gaze and retreated back inside the bar, disappearing into the gloomy interior. "You?"

"No." Colum shook his head.

"Come on." Shelby stepped past Colum in the direction of their car and climbed in. "The least we can do is see where they're going in such a hurry."

Colum followed her lead and jumped behind the wheel. He started the car and floored it, peeling away from the curb and speeding up to catch the vehicle that had just made a run at them.

The black sedan was still on the side road, where it slowed to within five miles of the speed limit. Colum caught up easily and sat on the vehicle's tail as it approached Main Street. "They have federal plates, just like us."

"Taking a photo of the plate now," Shelby said, lifting her phone, zooming, and snapping a picture through the windshield. "Got it."

"Well?" Colum glanced toward her.

"Don't know," Shelby said, looking at the photo. "G14 prefix."

"Am I supposed to know what that means?"

"All federal vehicles in the government fleet system use a white plate with blue lettering containing a prefix code to identify which department they're assigned to."

"Great. That helps us, right?"

"NOT SO MUCH." Shelby shook her head. "G14 is the code for vehicles assigned to the interagency motor pool. Any number of different agencies could be using that car."

"Dammit." Colum grimaced.

"Hey, at least we know it's government," Shelby said. "That's a start."

"It also means we're not the only Feds in town."

"We're not really Feds, remember?"

"You know what I mean."

Shelby rested the phone on her lap. "Maybe they aren't really Feds, either."

"Maybe." The car ahead of them was almost at the intersection. Colum gripped the wheel, sensing something was about to happen.

It slowed, as if about to stop, then barreled forward and took the corner at a reckless speed, proving his hunch right. The sedan's back end fishtailed for a moment and almost spun out, but the driver was good. He got it under control and sped away toward the outskirts of town.

"Dammit." Colum slammed his foot on the accelerator and matched their speed as he flew around the corner, braking into the turn and accelerating out of it.

Main Street was two lanes in each direction. The sedan weaved from one to the other, zipping around the slower traffic ahead of it.

Thankfully, traffic was light.

Colum pushed his own vehicle as fast as he dared and following behind, gaining on the sedan as it reached the outskirts of town. He rode their tail, looking for an opportunity to overtake, drop in front of them, and cut the black sedan off. But he couldn't risk it. There were just a few too many other cars, even after they left Blatchford in their rearview mirror.

The sedan sped up again, barreling along at close to twice the speed limit now.

"Wonder where they're going in such a hurry?" Shelby

already had the maps app open on her phone and was studying their surroundings. "There's nothing out here for miles but trees."

"I guess we keep on them and find out," Colum said, inching his own speed up. He had expected the car to turn onto Main in the direction they were originally heading, which would have taken them back toward the interstate. Instead, it had turned right and was now driving in an area of dense woodlands that sprawled over rugged hillsides on its way to vast tracts of state forest. "If they're hoping to lose us, they won't have much luck out here."

"Maybe they're not trying to lose us," Shelby said, twisting in her seat to look back through the rear windshield.

Colum lifted his gaze to the rear-view mirror and saw what she was referring to. Another car was coming up fast behind them. A police cruiser, no doubt with the Blatchford Sheriff's Office. The bar lights on its roof flicked on, flashing red and blue. Two quick bleats of the siren left no doubt regarding the cruiser's intentions.

"He's pulling us over," Shelby said, the disbelief clear in her voice. "Surely they must see that we have federal plates."

The cruiser had gained on them. Its siren sounded again.

"Apparently, they don't care." Colum's gaze shifted frontward again. The black sedan was pulling away, apparently unconcerned by the police vehicle sitting one car back on its tail. "If I stop, we lose them. Call Sheriff Clay and ask him to get that cruiser off our back."

Shelby closed the maps app and dialed, then switched to speaker.

It rang three times before the dispatcher answered.

Shelby identified herself as an FBI agent, using her cover name, then asked to be put through to Sheriff Clay.

"I'm sorry, Special Agent North, but Sheriff Clay is in a meeting can't be disturbed." The dispatcher did not sound sorry. In fact, she hesitated before replying and cleared her throat. An indicator that she was lying.

The police cruiser inched closer, it's siren on full blast now.

Colum glanced toward Shelby. "This is Special Agent Dale Winters. Put us through to Sheriff Clay right now. Get him out of that meeting if you have to."

Another pause on the other end of the line. "I can't do that. Perhaps you would like to speak with one of the deputies?"

"How about you radio the deputy who's currently trying to pull us over and tell them to back off." Colum didn't bother to hide the irritation in his voice. "We're on official Bureau business and following a suspect vehicle."

"Let me see what I can do," the dispatcher said. "Please hold."

There was a click, and the line went dead.

"Did she just hang up on us?" Shelby stared at the phone screen in disbelief.

"She did." Colum's gaze shifted from the black sedan to another police cruiser approaching them from the opposite direction. "And I think I know why."

"You've got to be kidding me."

The black sedan sped up again, increasing the gap between them. As it blew past, the police cruiser approaching from the other direction activated its light bar and swung across the road, blocking their way.

Colum swore and slammed on his brakes.

The car came to a skidding halt a mere ten feet from the cruiser, even as the deputy behind them stopped and exited his vehicle, gun drawn in the low ready position.

His companion in the other vehicle climbed out and approached from the opposite direction, his own gun similarly situated. Together they converged on Shelby and Colum.

Meanwhile, the black sedan kept going and was soon nothing but a spec on the road ahead. Then it was gone.

10

COLUM STORMED through the Sheriff's Department toward Sheriff Clay's office with Shelby a step behind. A harried desk sergeant raced to intercept them, a look of panic on his face, and stepped in front of the office door a moment before the Irishman reached it.

"Get out of my way," Colum growled, possessing enough forethought to slip into his American accent.

When the desk sergeant didn't immediately do as he was told, Colum reared to his full height, easily towering a foot above the man who blocked his path. He flexed his shoulders and fixed the sergeant with a steely gaze.

The officer looked up at him, no doubt trying to gauge how much peril he was in, then shrugged and stepped aside.

"That's better." Colum brushed past him and flung the sheriff's door open.

It banged back on its hinges, leaving a handle sized dent in the drywall.

Colum ignored the damage and stepped into the office,

then slammed the door closed as soon as Shelby had joined him.

Sheriff Clay was seated at his desk, hunched over an open manila folder. At the sudden interruption, his head jerked up. "You'd better have a damn good reason for storming in here like this, Special Agent Winters." He looked past Colum to Shelby. "The same goes for you, Special Agent North."

"How about a couple of Sheriff's Department cruisers chasing us down and getting in our way while we were following a suspect."

The Sheriff observed his uninvited guests for a long moment, then motioned to a pair of chairs on the other side of his desk. "Please, won't you sit down?"

"I'm fine right where I am." Colum folded his arms and returned the Sheriff's stare.

"Very well." Clay leaned back in his chair and sighed. "My deputies were just doing their job."

Shelby stepped forward, speaking quickly before Colum could answer. "Your deputies placed themselves between us and individuals who may know something about what's happening in your town."

"Nothing is happening in this town except a spree of unrelated incidents that my deputies are more than capable of handling. To be honest, I'm not sure why the two of you are even still here." Sheriff Clay put his hands behind his head. "I guess the FBI doesn't have any real crime to investigate."

"I can't tell if you're deliberately ignoring what's going on here, or if you really don't see it. Either way, it doesn't explain what just happened. Why were those deputies chasing us down?" Colum had asked the same thing of the police officers after he and Shelby had identified themselves as FBI agents. Neither man had answered. They merely apologized and beat a hasty retreat. After that, Colum continued down the road looking for the black sedan, but it was gone.

Sheriff Clay looked uncomfortable. "We received a request for backup from the state police. They said a pair of fugitives in a stolen car matching the description of your vehicle were on Route fifty-five north of town. Asked us to intercept and hold until they arrived."

"Except that we aren't fugitives, and our car has federal plates."

"I know, which is why my deputies backed off as soon as they confirmed your identities."

Colum was relieved that CUSP had done a good job setting up their false identities and making sure their cover would withhold scrutiny. "And the state police that were supposed to be on their way?"

"I think you know the answer to that."

"They never showed up."

"Correct. We tried to follow up and determine where the request came from, but the Staties didn't know what we were talking about."

"In other words, the request came from someone else."

"More than likely, whoever was responsible for the vehicle we were following," Shelby said. "They had government plates, too."

"You're berating me because my deputies stopped you, and meanwhile you were following another federal vehicle?" Clay raised an eyebrow. "Am I the only one who sees the irony in this?"

"The people in that car were not feds. At least, they weren't with our agency."

"And you know this how?"

"A hunch." Colum leaned on the desk. "Whether or not you like it, Sheriff Clay, something weird is going on in your town. The occupants of that car were tailing us, no doubt to see why we're in Blatchford and if we pose a threat to whatever they are doing. When we spotted them, they tried to run us down."

"Which is why we followed them. Thanks to your department, they got away." Shelby took her phone out and opened the photo she had taken earlier. She turned the screen toward the Sheriff. "But since we're here, you can do us a favor and run these plates. See which agency they belong to."

Sheriff Clay looked at the photo and then shook his head. "Not going to happen. I've already annoyed one bunch of Feds today. I don't need to make it two."

Colum shrugged. "I can have our people do it, but a little cooperation would go a long way in making up for what happened earlier."

Sheriff Clay stroked his chin in silence, then he grimaced. "Send me a copy of the photo and I'll see what I can do. No promises."

"Thank you." Colum watched as Shelby sent the photo to the department's email account. "You'll let us know as soon as it's done?"

"Sure. I only hope those plates don't turn out to be NSA or some other organization whose cage I don't want to rattle."

"Only one way to find out," Colum said. He didn't believe for a second that the car would come back as registered to the NSA. For one thing, the people tailing them were too sloppy. For another, the National Security Agency would never be so clumsy as to let covert operatives drive around in a vehicle that could be so easily traced back to them.

"Are we done here?" Sheriff Clay glanced at the door.

"I believe so." Colum turned to Shelby. "You got any more questions for the sheriff, Special Agent North?"

"I think we've covered the pertinent issues."

"My thoughts exactly." Colum opened the door for Shelby and waited for her to step through before following, with the Sheriff's eyes drilling into his back. As they made their way back outside, he wondered if Clay was as clueless as he made out, or if he already knew exactly who was in that car . . . and what they were up to.

11

AFTER THEY RETURNED to the hotel, Colum was restless. He paced back and forth in his room, hands pushed into his pockets.

"Will you quit that?" Shelby said, watching him from her chair at a table near the window.

"Sorry." Colum took a seat opposite her. "I don't feel like we're getting anywhere with this. That car with the federal plates got away, and Sheriff Clay is less than helpful. He doesn't think anything untoward is happening in his town."

"Or he does and has decided to leave well enough alone." Shelby looked thoughtful. "I can't imagine he has a hand in whatever is going on, he's just a small-town sheriff, but he could have been warned off digging too deep."

"If that's the case, we aren't going to hear back from him about that plate."

"You really think the Sheriff's Department received a tip about us from what they thought were the state police?"

"Hard to say." Colum shrugged. "But I do know that the

occupants of that car wanted us off their tail and had enough clout to have the local cops do it for them."

"Which means we're dealing with more than just the individuals in that car. Especially when you take the government plates into account."

"I agree. Although those plates could be fake just like ours."

"That doesn't preclude some shady government organization."

"No. It just means they don't want anyone finding out who they are." Colum rubbed his eyes. "Of course, this is all speculation. We have no proof of anything either way."

"Then let's get some." Shelby took out her phone. "Even if Sheriff Clay runs that plate—and that's a big if—there's no guarantee he'll tell us the truth regarding what he finds. I think it's time we took matters into our own hands."

"You want to send the plate number over to CUSP."

Shelby nodded. "They have the contacts to dig into this, and at least we'll get a straight answer."

"Do it." Colum preferred not to involve their employer during field operations if it wasn't necessary. Even though their phones and laptops were encrypted at the highest levels, nothing was totally secure. Sheriff Clay had mentioned the NSA. Was that just an innocent reference, or a slip of the tongue? If an organization like the National Security Agency was involved in the strange events occurring around town, CUSP's high-level encryption would mean nothing. An agency like that was probably monitoring their communications in real time and had the ability to crack even the most secure messages. Especially since the technology used to encode them probably came from the US

Government in the first place. On the other hand, they had no proof that any government agency was involved and there wasn't any other viable option, since they didn't trust the sheriff.

Shelby was hunched over her phone. She picked away at the screen, then looked up. "Done."

"Now all we can do is wait and see what they come back with." Another disturbing thought had occurred to Colum. If some shadowy government agency, either known or unknown, was operating in the area, they would probably be aware that Colum and Shelby were not real FBI agents. The legend set up for them by CUSP was good enough to convince local or even state police, but it wouldn't fool an agency like the NSA for long.

Shelby remained silent for a while, lost in her own thoughts, then she looked up at Colum. "If there is some secretive government agency operating in the area, do you think they're responsible for what's been going on in Blatchford, or are they investigating it just like us?"

"That's a good question." Colum hadn't considered that they weren't the only people drawn to Blatchford. Now he wanted to know who was in that car more than ever.

His laptop was on the table. Colum pulled the computer toward him and opened it, then brought up a map of the area around the town, including the road where they had followed the car with federal plates. Had it been heading to the destination along that route or deliberately going in the wrong direction until it could shake them?

He pored over the map, following the road past where they had been intercepted until he came to the next town but saw no obvious destinations. Going back to the starting point, Colum widened the search on the assumption that the car intended to double back but still found nothing that raised his suspicions. Even more frustrated than before, he closed the laptop and pushed it away again.

"Where do we go from here?" Shelby asked, observing Colum from across the desk.

"I don't know. We have no idea what the occupants of that car were doing here or where they were heading when we lost them. The Sheriff is less than helpful. The people caught up in the recent violence don't appear to have any more insight into their emotional outbursts than we do."

"Maybe it's like the sheriff claims," Shelby said. "Just a bunch of random acts that occurred during the same timeframe by coincidence."

"You don't believe that any more than I do." Colum drummed the fingers of his left hand on the desk. "And our employers certainly don't believe it, otherwise they wouldn't have sent us here. Whatever's happening is real."

"Well, we're not going to get any more answers today." Shelby glanced out the window toward the parking lot. "We pretty much exhausted our lines of inquiry."

Colum knew she was right. They probably wouldn't even get any information back from CUSP on the license plate before morning. He glanced at his watch. It was already seven in the evening and his stomach was growling. "Want to get some dinner, and maybe a pint at whatever passes for the local pub in these parts?"

"I thought you'd never ask." Shelby grinned. "Are you buying?"

"Sure. Why not. It's all going on the expense account, anyway."

"Great." Shelby stood up and started toward the door

connecting their rooms. "Give me ten minutes to take a shower, and I'm all yours."

"Sounds like a plan." Colum watched her go, then opened the laptop again to see what culinary delights the town of Blatchford had to offer.

12

JACKSON ROOKE WAS in the living room of his one-story ranch house sitting by the fire and reading a book when he heard the horses whinnying in the barn.

He lowered the book and listened. This was not the brief and low contented neighing they usually engaged in. This was longer. Higher pitched. A whinny of distress... or fear.

Rooke threw the book down on the couch and jumped up, grabbing his shotgun from a rack near the front door even as he pulled his coat on. He pulled the door open and stepped outside, ignoring the chill night air, and started toward the horse barn, his gaze roaming the landscape around the house for any sign of danger. Like a coyote, or a fox that had strayed too close and alarmed the eight steeds in the squat and low building that occupied a footprint bigger than his own dwelling.

He saw nothing.

No low and menacing silhouettes, the telltale sign of nocturnal predators on the hunt, slinking across the paddocks or sniffing around the horse barn, whose doors remained securely closed. Nothing had ventured inside. At least, nothing big enough to scare a horse.

Another round of whinnying rose from the barn.

Rooke stopped in his tracks, lifting the shotgun even though he still could not see a threat. Maybe it wasn't another animal that had scared the horses, but a human . . . Which meant there might be an intruder inside the barn after all. He raced toward the doors and flung one open, stepping inside, and reaching for the light switch even as he brought the gun up.

The barn comprised a central alleyway, with five horse stalls to the left and five more to the right. Beyond this was an open area where the feed and saddles were stored.

Rooke stood in the doorway, the hairs on the back of his neck prickling.

The closest horse, a mare named Isabel, gave a high-pitched whine, and looked at him, her brown eyes glistening.

"It's okay, girl," Rooke said, reaching out and placing a calming hand on her head.

She stomped a foot and whined again, joining in with a chorus of whinnies from the other animals.

Rooke took a step forward, moving deeper into the barn and checking each stall as he passed. He reached the far side of the building and another set of doors. These were closed, too. Rooke came to a stop and looked around, confused. The horses were still distressed, but he could see no reason for it.

Maybe the threat wasn't inside the barn, but somewhere beyond its walls. Lowering the gun, he stepped back outside and closed the door before circling to the front of the barn again and gazing out across the paddocks toward the woods that ringed his thirty-acre property.

At first, Rooke saw nothing amiss, but then he caught

movement out of the corner of his eye. A subtle shift in the darkness. But it didn't come from the forest, or even the barn. It was higher. He lifted his gaze to the sky and finally understood what had spooked the horses.

Six points of light hovered over the barn, forming a circle. There was no sound. He could see no structure between them, nothing to indicate whether the lights were all attached to one larger craft, or six individual units.

The breath caught in Rooke's throat.

He reeled off the possibilities in his head. A helicopter? No. He couldn't hear the steady chop of rotor blades or feel the downwash from the hovering craft. And it wasn't a plane, because planes didn't sit motionless in the sky like that. Which left only one possibility.

Rooke lifted the shotgun even as he staggered back, away from the strange object that was terrifying his horses.

He pulled the trigger. Pulled it again.

The twin shotgun blasts were deafening but didn't appear to have any effect on whatever was hanging motionless in the sky above him.

Unsure what to do next, he stood and watched. If it weren't for the horses, Rooke would have turned tail and fled. Run as fast as he could back to the house and barricaded himself inside, because he'd seen enough of those shows on TV to know what had invaded his meager plot of airspace.

It was a UFO.

Because what else could it be?

Rooke glanced around, nervous. He half expected to see strange and elongated figures with pear-shaped heads and bulging eyes appear out of the darkness to spirit him away.

Or maybe they already had.

Rooke checked his watch and was relieved to find that it

was only fifteen minutes later than when he left the house. Not enough time to be abducted and returned.

But that didn't mean he was safe.

In fact, the longer he stood there, the longer he risked something bad happening.

Rooke spared another thought for the horses, then decided they were safe enough in the barn. He backed away slowly, keeping the gun pointed upward toward the strange object.

As if sensing his retreat, the lights moved. They spun counterclockwise and peeled off one by one until, instead of a circle, they had formed a line across the sky. They were moving now, too. But not toward Rooke.

They flew silently over the horse paddocks toward the woods. Then, as if they had disturbed some sleeping monster, an undulating black swarm rose from between the trees like a living blanket and took to the sky, momentarily blocking his view of the lights.

A whimper escaped Rooke's throat. He couldn't tell what he was looking at, but it disturbed him on some primordial level. Without waiting to see what would happen next, he turned and fled back to the house until he arrived at the wraparound porch. He took the steps two at a time and tugged on his front door, yanking it open and almost tumbling across the threshold.

When he turned to close the door, his eyes lifted to the sky once more, but nothing was there now. The lights were gone, and so was the strange black swarm. Only the nervous cries of his horses remained as proof that anything strange had occurred.

13

COLUM AND SHELBY drove back into Blatchford and parked up outside the only ethnic eatery in town—unless you counted the Taco Bell on the east end of Main Street.

The Thai Palace restaurant stood on a corner two blocks from the Sheriff's Department. Colum had seen it earlier in the day and made a mental note of its location. Later, he checked it out on YELP while Shelby was taking a shower. It scored a whopping six five-star reviews and a single one-star that complained about the gruff service, but he figured it was still a notch above the greasy hamburger and fries that waited for them at the fast-food places out by the interstate.

"This actually isn't too bad," Shelby said in a surprised tone after Colum held the door open for her to enter. She looked around, taking in the deep red painted walls, original plank floors, and a string of chandeliers that hung over the tables and bathed the dining room in a pleasant glow that was bright enough to see by, but not garish. "Kind of cute and romantic."

"Don't get any ideas," Colum said, as the hostess led them

to a booth at the back of the restaurant. "You start getting all doe eyed and I'm driving us back to Mickey-D's for a couple of quarter pounders."

"That doesn't sound like the Colum I worked with in Prague. As I remember, you used that Irish charm to your full advantage, even though barely anyone there understood what you were saying. I seem to recall there was one particular young lady—"

"Helenka." Colum smiled at the memory. "That was different. She wasn't on the payroll. I don't get involved with coworkers. Too messy."

"Well, pardon me." Shelby pulled a face. "And for your information, I wasn't intending to get all doe eyed. As for Prague, I was merely commenting on your well-earned reputation."

"Well, okay then." Colum wasn't sure if he was relieved or offended. He leaned forward. "And FYI, I think we should maintain our cover while we're out in public."

"Sure thing, *Dale*." Shelby flashed a quick grin, But Colum was distracted. He was staring past her through the restaurant's front window. She reached out and tapped his arm. "Hey. What's wrong?"

"The car from earlier. The one with the federal plates." Colum was already sliding from the booth. "It's here, parked up outside."

"You think it followed us here?" Shelby swiveled around to look.

"Either that or they're picking up a takeout order of Pad Thai and have incredibly bad timing." Colum was on his feet and heading toward the door. He pulled it open and stepped outside.

The black sedan stood at the curb on the opposite side of

the street. It was night and the vehicle's windows were tinted, making it impossible to see the occupants.

Colum was wearing his Glock in a shoulder holster under his jacket. He kept his hands in sight but was ready to reach for it at a moment's notice should the situation turn hostile. He started toward the vehicle.

He'd only taken a couple of steps when the sedan's engine revved, and it pulled away from the curb. For a moment the vehicle stopped in the road, brake lights glowing red, as if the driver wanted to see what would happen next. Then, as Colum drew close enough to reach for the passenger door handle, the black sedan rolled forward and picked up speed, disappearing down Main Street at a clip and was soon swallowed up by the night.

Colum stood in the road and watched it go. When he turned back toward the restaurant, Shelby was standing on the sidewalk.

"Guess they weren't picking up Pad Thai."

"Guess not." Colum stomped past Shelby and pulled the restaurant door open. "I'm starving. Let's eat."

14

As COLUM and Shelby were heading toward town and their encounter with the black sedan outside the Thai Palace restaurant, another vehicle was heading in the opposite direction toward the woods. It was a red SUV with a sticker on the rear bumper that read 'Proud parents of a straight-A student at Blatchford High'. But there were no parents in the vehicle. Not tonight. Instead, it was the straight-A student herself sitting behind the wheel. Josie Anne Jordan.

The seventeen-year-old had gotten her license three months before and had been told in no uncertain terms that her own ride would not be forthcoming unless she maintained her grades and graduated high school with honors the following year. Which was why she was stuck with the family SUV and not the two-seater Miata of her dreams. Which was just as well, because right now there were three of her best friends in the car, all of whom Josie had picked up outside the library after telling her parents she was going there to study.

Maddie sat in the front passenger seat; eyes glued to her phone as usual. At least until the signal dropped, which it always did about five miles outside of town.

"Dammit," Maddie said, her voice heavy with disappointment. "I was in the middle of tweeting about the party."

From the backseat, their friend Hannah snorted. "That's so smart. Tell everyone we're heading out to a party in the woods when our parents think we're in the library studying."

"Would you relax?" Maddie turned to peer through the gap between the front seats. "None of our parents know how to find us on social media, let alone follow us."

"Mine do," said Bobby Gordon, Hannah's boyfriend, and the star quarterback at Blatchford High. "They've been following me for a couple of years."

"OMG. You just thought to mention this now?" Maddie huffed and turned frontward again, then folded her arms.

"Hey, what can I say?" Bobby grinned. "They take an interest in what I do."

"More like they're snooping on you."

"Don't talk to Bobby like that." Hannah leaned forward and flicked Maddie's ear.

"Ow. What the hell?"

"You deserved it."

"Hey, cut it out, guys. We're almost there." Josie steered the SUV off the main highway and onto a smaller single lane road with cracked and heaving asphalt that ran through the woods to a local historic site and sometimes teen hangout known as Witches Hollow.

When they arrived, there were already several other cars parked in the pull off, beyond which a dark and gloomy trail led deeper into the woods.

They climbed out and Josie went to the trunk where she grabbed a bottle of wine liberated from her parent's small stash they kept hidden in their cellar. "Don't want to forget the alcohol."

"Dang right." Bobby reached past her and grabbed a sixpack of beer.

Josie closed the trunk and set off up the trail with the others following behind. After a few minutes, the trees thinned, and they found themselves in a large clearing with a set of stone ruins in the middle. The remains of what had once been a pioneer cabin and several smaller structures.

A bonfire burned in the middle of the clearing, its flames leaping into the evening sky and sending dancing embers spiraling toward the heavens on the updraft like a thousand orange fireflies. Around the fire were clusters of figures in silhouette. At least thirty of them. All students at Blatchford High.

"That looks safe," Josie said, eyeing the pyre.

"Lighten up." Hannah snatched the wine bottle from Josie's hand and twisted it open. "Good. You brought a screw top this time."

"Hey. That wasn't me." Josie scrunched her nose. "I always bring a screw top."

"It was Maddie," Bobby said as they approached a fallen log and sat on it. He grabbed a beer and popped the top, taking a swig before speaking again.

Maddie glared at him. "We found a corkscrew, didn't we?"

"Yeah. Because we were at Barry Dunham's house. Good luck finding one out here."

Josie smiled. She remembered the incident well. Barry's

parents were out of town for the weekend, and he threw one of the more memorable parties of the summer. It felt so long ago now winter had come and they were back in school, even though it was less than four months before. She reached out and grabbed the bottle from Hannah. "My turn."

"Don't hog that." Hannah eyed her friend as she gulped a mouth full of wine.

"That's why I'm drinking beer," Maddie said, taking a bottle from the sixpack.

"Yuck." Hannah pulled the face.

"What, are you too good for beer?" Maddie grinned.

"No, I just don't like it, that's all."

Maddie started to reply, her eyes glinting with mischief, but then a strange expression came upon her. The grin fell away to be replaced with a sneer. She put the beer down and stood up. "Speaking of being too good, Bobby deserves better than you."

"What?" Hannah jumped to her feet. Her face flushing red with anger.

"Hey, what's going on?" Josie stepped between them, confused at this sudden outburst from her friends.

"You heard me." Maddie scowled. "Bobby's too good for you. He deserves better."

"You mean like you?" Hannah tried to sidestep Josie.

"Sure. I am better for him. He told me so last week."

"He said no such thing."

"Really? Where do you think he was last Wednesday night?"

"Studying." Hannah's voice faltered. "At least, that's what he told me."

"Yeah, well, he lied."

"Stop." Bobby dropped his beer and leaped up. He turned to Hannah. "I was studying. I swear."

Maddie laughed. "I wouldn't call what we were up to studying. But hey..."

"I hate you." Hannah flew forward, pushing Josie aside. She barreled into Maddie and the pair tumbled to the ground in a tangle of flailing limbs.

Bobby stood watching, mouth agape. "I swear, I wasn't with Maddie last week. I've never been with Maddie."

But Josie wasn't listening. Because Maddie and Hannah weren't the only ones locked in confrontation. Around the bonfire, at least three other fights were underway. Shouts of anger mixed with shocked screams floated on the chill November breeze.

A girl with long blonde hair fled toward the parking lot with another girl in hot pursuit.

Two of Bobby's friends—both on the football team—got into the action, taking swings at each other between loudly voiced obscenities while a girl with long auburn hair filmed the encounter with a gleeful look on her face. Josie recognized her as another Blatchford High senior named Gemma Ward.

And then Josie noticed something else. A low thrum that sounded like a distant train, even though there were no train tracks anywhere close to Blatchford.

The rumble grew louder, a cacophony of drumbeats that sounded like... beating wings.

Josie raised her eyes to the sky, and the pale quarter moon that peeked through a break in the clouds. There was something else, too. Another light, pale white and silent, that hovered above the trees. No, scratch that. More than one light hovering in a tight formation . . . at least until an undulating black shape blotted it out.

Except it wasn't one shape. It was thousands of small black shapes that flitted and circled in confused agitation.

Josie screamed and lifted her hands to protect her face, even as the agitated tide of bats swooped into the clearing and enveloped her in a flurry of squirming, flapping bodies.

15

IT WAS SATURDAY MORNING. Colum had risen early, as was his habit thanks to so many years in the military, and stepped out to find coffee, figuring that Shelby would not yet be awake. There was a Starbucks near the interstate, and he headed there, picking up two large lattes.

When he got back, Shelby was up. He could hear her moving around in the adjoining room and knocked on the connecting door. When he entered, she was sitting at the table in front of the window with her laptop open.

Colum held up one of the lattes. "I brought coffee."

"Starbucks. Nice."

"Figured it would perk us up." Colum settled on the chair opposite her. "I heard back from CUSP. They made some discreet inquiries into that Federal plate."

"And?"

"Nothing. Not assigned to any department or agency that anyone knew about. In fact, the plate number doesn't even officially exist. Or if it does, someone scrubbed it from the record."

"Which means that whoever is using that car wants to stay anonymous."

"Yes. Has all the hallmarks of black ops." Colum leaned forward. "What are you up to?"

Shelby sipped her coffee before replying, then smacked her lips in appreciation. "I needed that." She turned the computer so they could both see the screen. "I've been monitoring social media. Figured there might have been more strange incidents than Sheriff Clay knows about. Smaller stuff not worth reporting to the cops but interesting enough to tweet or post about."

"You can do that?" Colum pulled the lid off his coffee.

Shelby nodded. "Sure. There's a bunch of monitoring tools out there."

"Huh. I guess the government really is watching everything we say and do."

"Nothing so nefarious. It's all above board. Brands and influencers use them to track social awareness. Political campaigns can track sentiment during election cycles. Even regular people use them to find topics of interest. Not that agencies like the FBI don't have access to even more advanced tracking tools. I bet CUSP employs similar technology to monitor strange events around the world."

"Probably," Colum said. "But that's a bit outside my sphere of expertise. I just go where they send me and do what they ask. Is that what you're using, some deep state tracker software?"

Shelby laughed. "Hardly. I downloaded it yesterday morning and signed up for a one-month free trial. All above board. Didn't even need to find my way onto the dark web. Even you could have done it."

"I wouldn't count on that. Social media isn't exactly my

DEADLY TRUTH

thing." Colum leaned forward to look at the screen. "Did you find anything?"

"Not at first. All I got was the usual inane crap that people think it's okay to share with the world. Brenda615 loves baking apple pies, and apparently photographing them to prove it. Jordan hoped her Friday evening was going to be #SoRomantic. And Emma thinks her week was the 'worst ever . . . so stressed' without providing any context, but still managed to get forty replies sympathizing with her unnamed plight and telling her to 'power through it, girl' among other things."

"And that's why I don't bother with social media," Colum said with a grin. "It's inane."

"Right. But then I got this from a girl named Maddie. She's a senior at Blatchford high." Shelby brought up a tweet.

'Party tonight. See you at Witches Hollow. #seniorfun.'

Colum read the tweet. "What's Witches Hollow?"

"It's a local historical landmark out in the woods a couple of miles from town. A clearing with the ruins of a Pioneer era cabin. Local legend says a witch named Abigail Fenton lived there until she was dragged outside and burned at the stake. She's supposed to be buried somewhere in the woods in an unmarked grave. And get this . . . With her dying breath, she cursed the town."

"Naturally." Colum chuckled. "I bet she haunts the clearing, too."

"How did you know?"

"Lucky guess."

"Of course, that particular legend should probably taken with a grain of salt. Apparently, local teenagers] been using it as a party spot for generations and you k how teens love to make up ghost stories."

"Can't be much of a historical landmark if they let high schoolers use it to make out and party."

"I guess the town would like to forget their witch burning past."

"Don't blame them." Colum paused. "So how do a bunch of teens partying in the woods figure into what's going on in Blatchford?"

"Because that tweet wasn't all I found." Shelby brought up another post with a video attached. "Watch this."

She pressed play.

The video started with a bunch of teens drinking and chatting around a roaring bonfire. It was dark. Music was playing. Someone passed in front of the camera, momentarily turning the image black. There was a fuzzy shot of a beer bottle.

Then a scream followed by several excited shouts.

The camera panned left.

A fight had broken out between two boys wearing letterman jackets. They swung at each other, mostly missing the mark amid shoves and jeers.

Another scream, this one more urgent. Then two more. High-pitched and full of terror.

The image shifted in a blur of movement as whoever was behind the phone searched for the source of the consternation. Finally, the would-be cinematographer found their subject. A tide of small creatures that soared out of the sky into the clearing in a cascade of beating wings. Thousands of them. The person holding the phone let out a terrified screech. A hand flashed in front of the lens as if the person holding the phone was trying to fend off the arial assault. A puckered, gargoyle-like face with beady red eyes filled the screen before a thud sent the image tumbling wildly.

The phone had obviously been knocked from its operator's hands and now lay on the ground. A low angle view of panicked teenagers fleeing the onslaught of winged creatures was suddenly cut off when a hand scooped the phone up again. A moment later, the screen went black, and the video ended.

Colum sat in silence for a moment, then drew in a long breath. "Bats. Thousands of bats."

"Right." Shelby sat back in her chair. "Bats that have worked themselves into a frenzy."

"And appear to have lost their ability to avoid obstacles."

"Echolocation," Shelby said. "Bats use ultrasound to navigate and they're very good at it. Apparently these particular bats, not so much."

"Or maybe something was interfering with their natural abilities." Colum leaned his elbows on the table. "Can you rewind the footage to the moment before the bats appear?"

"Sure." Shelby went back to where the fight broke out. She hit play.

Colum watched for a moment as the camera's field-of-view arched upwards toward the sky and the approaching bats, then slapped the table. "Did you see that?"

"See what?"

"Go back again."

Shelby pulled the video back several frames and let it run forward again.

"Pause it there," Colum said quickly.

Shelby paused the video. The bats froze mid swoop. Behind them, higher in the sky, was a fuzzy white light.

"What is that?" Shelby narrowed her eyes. "A plane passing overhead, or maybe a helicopter?"

"I don't think so. If they were running lights, there should also be red and green beacons. All I see is white."

"You think it has a connection to the bats' odd behavior?"

"Hard to say. It could be anything. It might even be an out-of-focus shot of the moon because the camera was trying to focus on much closer objects."

"I don't think so," said Shelby. She ran the footage again. As the camera panned back down, another pale white object came into view. This time, it was recognizable. The moon.

"Well, that rules one theory out." Colum scratched his chin. "Can you find out who took this video?"

"Probably." Shelby turned the laptop back toward her.

"Good. Do it." Colum folded his arms. "And then I think it's time for FBI agents Winters and North to have a chat with our amateur filmmaker."

16

It didn't take long for Shelby to find out who had shot the bat video and get her home address. It was a seventeen-year-old senior from Blatchford High. Gemma Ward.

"People should be more careful with their online identity," Shelby said, as they headed out the door to go see the girl. "It's too easy to track people down. Phone numbers. Email addresses. Street address. Even Social Security numbers and other supposedly private information are all out there if you know where to look. The internet is like a stalker's paradise these days."

"Sometimes you scare me," Colum said as they reached the car and climbed in.

"Hey, I'm just calling it as I see it." Shelby buckled her seatbelt. "I spent a year in the cyber-crimes division of the FBI. It would amaze you what goes on."

"I'm not sure I want to know." Colum pulled out of the hotel parking lot. "I've tried to avoid the seedy underbelly of humanity since I left the military."

"Yet you're quite happy to chase down all sorts of violent

supernatural creatures the rest of the world barely believes in anymore."

"That's different."

"I don't see how. My visit to The Zoo when I first joined CUSP gave me nightmares for weeks. The things they're keeping in that place..."

"I put a few of those things there myself," Colum said.

"You think what's going on here is supernatural?" Shelby asked.

"Right now, I don't know what to think. How far outside town is that place where the kids were partying?"

"Witch's Hollow."

"Right. There."

"Not sure. Why?"

"Figure we should pay a visit to the scene and check it out before we go visit our filmmaker."

"I'll get directions." Shelby unlocked her phone. "Just to be clear. You don't believe the witch has anything to do with this, right?"

"Absolutely. A witch's curse and a town plagued by crazy incidents. What else could it be?"

"You're teasing me, aren't you?"

"Just a little bit. But we shouldn't rule something out simply because it sounds far-fetched. I learned that lesson early on with CUSP."

"Okay, then. Not discounting the witch theory." Shelby tapped on her phone screen. "I have the directions. Looks like we have to turn right at the next intersection and then it's a couple of miles up on the left."

She propped the phone up in the center console and fell silent while it guided them to the clearing.

When they arrived, Colum pulled off the road and parked

next to a narrow trail that weaved between the trees. A wooden sign had been tacked to a post, pointing up the trail. A square metal plaque mounted on a pole stood on the other side of the trail entrance.

After getting out of the car, Colum walked over to the plaque and saw that it told the tale of the doomed witch, Abigail Fenton. Everything pretty much matched the story Shelby had relayed to him, except it didn't mention the curse or the ruins of the witch's cabin being haunted. He wondered if those details were simply embellishments added later to spice up the local lore. He hadn't seen much evidence of tourism in Blatchford, but figured a witch's curse couldn't hurt.

"You ready?" Shelby asked, standing near the trail entrance.

"Lead the way." Colum stepped away from the sign.

They walked up the trail under a canopy of tree branches and emerged into a flat area devoid of undergrowth. Someone had pulled logs into the clearing to serve as makeshift benches. A stone chimney and the remains of what must once have been the cabin walls stood in the middle of the space. The remains of a bonfire still smoldered, an occasional wisp of smoke curling up on the breeze.

"Damn kids are lucky they didn't start a forest fire," Colum said, eyeing the charred logs. "You think Sheriff Clay knows about this?"

"If he does, he didn't do much to break it up." Shelby was strolling the perimeter of the site. She kneeled and motioned for Colum to join her. "Come look at this."

Colum crossed to where she had stopped and saw what had attracted her attention. A small black body with leathery wings. It was lying on its back, ugly snub-nosed face peering lifelessly into the sky. "A dead bat."

Shelby climbed to her feet and took a few more steps. "There's another one here."

It didn't take long for Colum to find a third and a fourth bat. All of them were dead. He figured that if they searched the rest of the clearing, they would find more of the creatures.

He shuddered. "You know, in some cultures, bats were seen as familiars for witches just like black cats. Some even believe that witches could turn into bats, in much the same manner as the vampires of Eastern European folklore."

"Witches can't turn into bats," Shelby said. "And vampires aren't real."

"I hate to spoil your day, but we have no idea what witches can or cannot do," Colum replied. "And as for vampires, I assure you, they are most definitely real."

"Really?" Shelby raised an eyebrow. "I don't recall seeing one during my tour of The Zoo."

"Just because we aren't keeping one in captivity doesn't mean they aren't out there." An image of Mina popped into Colum's head. He was at her side when Abraham Turner, otherwise known as Jack the Ripper, had been dispatched by John Decker. Turner was about as close to a vampire as Colum ever wanted to meet. He used the blood of his victims to extend his own life. At least until that life force had ended up flowing into Mina.

Colum forced the image from his mind and focused back on the present. He strode toward the ruined cabin and looked around. "The video must have been taken somewhere right around here. You could see the ruins in some of the shots."

Shelby crossed to join him. "I don't see anything here that can help us." She nudged another dead bat with the toe of her shoe.

"I agree." Colum glanced up. He could see a patch of cloudy sky above the trees circling the edge of the clearing. "There can't have been many clouds last night. We could see the moon in that video."

Shelby followed his gaze. "You're wondering what that other light in the sky was."

"Aren't you?"

"Yes. But like you said, there was no cloud cover. That light could have been an object within twenty feet of the ground, or it could have been something much higher that was simply out of focus, which could have made it appear bigger. It might not even have had anything to do with what happened here."

"Or it might have everything to do with it." Colum turned back toward the trail. "But we're not going to find those answers here. Let's go have a chat with Gemma Ward."

17

GEMMA WARD'S home was a small single-story Cape Cod style building with a steep gable roof. When Colum and Shelby pulled up, there was a man, no doubt Gemma's father, clearing leaves with a rake. When he saw the car pull up he stopped and stood watching with his hands pushed into his pockets until they approached the front gate.

"Mister Ward?" Colum asked, slipping into his American accent.

"Who wants to know?" The man approached the gate with a wary look on his face.

Colum held up his fake ID and waited for Shelby to do the same. "I'm Special Agent Dale Winters with the FBI. This is my partner, Emily North."

"I see. What can I do for the pair of you?"

"Not you. Your daughter." Shelby slipped her credentials back into her pocket. "Is she here?"

"Yeah. She's here. Grounded after sneaking out to a party last night. She in some sort of trouble?"

"No." Shelby shook her head. "We just have some questions for her regarding that party."

"The FBI are investigating teenagers drinking in the woods now?"

"Underage drinking is a crime," Colum said with a blank expression.

"Seems like the federal government's resources would be better spent solving real crimes." Ward made no move to let them onto his property.

"You're not the first person who's told us that recently." Colum placed a hand on the gate. He glanced toward the house. "Would you mind?"

Ward sighed and stepped away from the gate. "You sure she's not in trouble? Because if she is, I should probably call a lawyer—"

"There won't be any need for lawyers, Mr. Ward," Shelby said. "We just have a few questions about something your daughter may have witnessed. She isn't under investigation, I promise you."

Ward observed Shelby and Colum in silence for a few moments, then shrugged. "In that case, I'll take you to her."

He turned and started up the path toward the front door. Colum let Shelby go first and then followed behind.

The Ward residence was small, with a living room front left and a kitchen dining room combination on the other side. The place wasn't a complete mess, but it wasn't exactly tidy, either. Colum sensed the absence of a woman's touch.

"Where's Mrs. Ward?" he asked after stepping inside.

"Damned if I know. Divorced." There was a sour edge to Ward's voice. "Took off with some guy she met over the internet two years ago."

"Sorry to hear that."

"Yeah. It happens." Ward led them toward the back of the house and the bedrooms. He knocked on a closed door. "Gemma, honey, there are some people here to see you."

There was no response from inside the room.

Ward knocked again. When his daughter still didn't respond, he grabbed the door handle and twisted, pushing the door open wide enough to peek inside.

This time he got a response.

Gemma was lying on the bed, eyes glued to her phone. There were several Band-Aids covering scratches on her face. She leaped up with a scowl and glared at her father. "What are you doing barging in on me?"

Ward pushed the door wider and stepped aside for Colum and Shelby. "These people are here to see you."

The look of annoyance fell from Gemma's face to be replaced by one of wary surprise. "Who are you?"

Colum held up his ID. "FBI."

"Is this about the party last night? Because I had nothing to do with those fights."

Colum stepped into the room and waited for Shelby to enter. He fixed the elder Ward with a hard stare until the man huffed and retreated to the front of the house, then turned his attention back to Gemma. "The fight you posted on social media wasn't the only one?"

Gemma shook her head. "There were at least three others. It was weird. One minute everyone was having fun, and the next they were trying to punch each other out." She sat on the edge of the bed and looked up at the fake FBI agents. "At least until the other thing happened."

"The bats."

"Yes." Gemma shuddered.

"Do you know what started the fights?"

"I know what started the one I filmed. Danny Travers accused Parker Donovan of cheating to get the starting wide receiver position."

"Cheating, how?"

Gemma shrugged. "Beats me. Drugs?"

"You mean like steroids," Colum said.

"There were rumors last semester that a few of the guys on the team took them. I guess Danny thought Parker was one of those people."

"And he waited until last night at a party to air that opinion?"

"I guess."

"Was there animosity between them before that?"

Gemma shrugged again. "Not so far as I know. I thought they were best friends. They were laughing and joking ten seconds before Danny Travers started throwing punches. It was like Danny just snapped."

"What happened next?"

"The bats came. It was like they appeared out of nowhere. Thousands of them. They were flying into us. Bouncing off of us." Gemma lifted a hand to her face, and the scratches. "I was lucky. Managed to avoid the worst of it. Some of the others got cut up and bruised real bad. It was insane. I've never seen anything like it."

"Apart from the fights, nothing happened before the bats appeared?" Colum asked. "You didn't see or hear anything that might have caused them to swarm like that?"

"Not really. When I looked at the video later there was a light in the sky, but I don't remember seeing it at the time. I was too busy trying to avoid the bats." Gemma looked up at Colum. "I know we shouldn't have been partying there, but the team just played in the championship last weekend and we wanted to celebrate their win. It's a tradition that has been going on forever when the team has a big win. You're not going to arrest me, are you?"

"You don't need to worry about that," said Shelby. "Last time I checked partying in high school wasn't exactly a federal offense. Besides, your dad said he grounded you. Sounds like he has your punishment under control. I assume you didn't tell him about the party?"

Gemma shook her head. "Because I knew he wouldn't let me go, even though he told me stories about parties he went to when he was in high school. Kind of feels like a double standard."

Shelby smiled. "I'm sure you'll enforce that same double standard when you have kids."

"If I ever get the chance. He might keep me locked up in this room until I'm sixty."

"I doubt that." Shelby touched Colum's arm and tilted her head toward the door. A silent signal that she thought they should leave. "But you might want to tell your dad you're sorry."

"You think he'll let me out of here any quicker if I do?" Gemma asked hopefully.

"Probably not."

Gemma looked down at the floor in glum resignation. "That's what I thought."

18

As they drove away from the Ward residence, Shelby looked at Colum. "You got any theories about what's going on here, yet?"

Colum kept his eyes on the road ahead. "Not an inkling. But whatever has been going on in this town happened out at that party last night. Gemma mentioned several fights breaking out all at once. It fits the pattern."

"There were no reports of any disturbances in town." Shelby was browsing the web. "At least, if there were, they didn't make the news."

"More to the point, Sheriff Clay didn't call us. Not that I find it surprising. I get the impression he's not exactly pleased with our presence here."

"Which is odd. You'd think the man would be happy for the FBI's help." Shelby lowered the phone to her lap. "You think he knows about what happened out in the woods?"

"It's a small town." Colum was heading toward Main Street. "We could stop by and ask him."

"What good would that do? If he knew about the incident out at Witch's Hollow, he didn't think to tell us."

"And if he didn't know about it, then he's not a very good Sheriff. After all, regardless of whatever else happened, half the senior class of Blatchford High were partying in the woods and he's sitting with his feet up on the desk clueless?"

"Sounds like it's a tradition in these parts. Maybe he knew about it but just didn't care." Shelby grimaced. "The thing I don't get is the bats. If something is affecting the citizens of this town, like poisoned drinking water or some sort of gas leak turning people randomly nuts, where does a swarm of bats fit in?"

"That's a good question. Maybe it's a—"

"Don't say coincidence. I don't believe that any more than you do."

"I wasn't going to say it was a coincidence. And you're right, I don't believe those bats happened to swarm like that all on their own. Whatever affected those high school kids also spooked the bats."

"And caused them to lose their ability to navigate," Shelby said. "Did you see the scratches on that girl's face?"

"Not to mention how many bats were dead on the ground up there. They were either completely disoriented, or so terrified that they flew into tree trunks." Colum took a long breath. "Maybe the witch's curse isn't so far-fetched."

"I was wondering how long it would take to come back around to that."

"Don't get me wrong, I'm not suggesting it really was a witch's curse, but you have to admit, the whole thing feels kind of spooky." Colum turned onto Main Street. "Maybe we shouldn't discount a supernatural angle."

"Okay. Give it your best shot. What kind of supernatural creature could be causing this?"

Colum hesitated a moment before applying. "If it weren't for the bats, my best guess would be a demon or some other type of non-corporeal entity possessing people and forcing them to act on their neuroses."

"Except that even if we assume possession is a real thing —and that's a big if—how could a demon possess more than one person at the same time?"

"My name is Legion, for we are many. Mark 5:9."

"Very good." Shelby looked suitably impressed. "Let me guess. Your Irish upbringing?"

"Five years of Catholic school and four times as many growing up in a Catholic household with a mother who really wanted me to be a priest. It leaves an impression."

"I bet." Shelby glanced sideways at Colum. "Can I ask you a question? In all your years working for CUSP, and with everything you've seen, have you ever actually encountered a demon? I mean an actual biblical demon from Hades, let alone a whole devilish convention of them hell-bent on possessing multiple people at the same time."

A wry smile creased Colum's lips. "Thankfully, no. But just because I haven't encountered something doesn't mean it isn't real."

"I agree." Shelby was tapping on her phone again. "But I don't think this is a case of demonic possession. It just doesn't fit the bill. But I'm damned if I can think what else it could be."

"And therein lies the problem." They were coming up to a red light. Colum slowed to a stop. "Given the unconventional nature of our job, is almost impossible to predict the nature of the threat. Hell, for all I know, it could be a Bigfoot causing all the trouble."

"I think we can safely rule out Bigfoot."

"You know what I mean."

"I do. Even though I still struggle to believe it most of the time." Shelby looked thoughtful. "You think there's something to the witch legend and the curse?"

"No. Not for a second. If there were, why would she wait a couple a hundred years to make her presence felt? This feels more... immediate."

"Still doesn't help us. What could cause random people to turn on each other, some of whom were best of friends a few minutes before, and also send thousands of bats into a mindless frenzy?"

Colum didn't have a good answer, supernatural or otherwise. But thankfully, he was spared a response because his phone rang. Taking one hand off the wheel, he pulled it from his pocket. It was Sheriff Clay.

He answered.

The Sheriff's deep voice boomed from the handset. "Special Agent Winters. I hope you don't mind me calling, but I have a lead that I think you'll find interesting. A farmer outside of town reported strange lights over his property yesterday evening. Seems like it will be just up your alley."

"What kind of strange lights?" Colum asked.

"The kind they usually class as UFOs," Clay replied, the amusement in his voice self-evident. "Since the pair of you are willing to entertain any scenario, no matter how far-fetched, I thought you might like to check it out."

"That's mighty magnanimous of you, Sheriff," Colum said with gritted teeth. "How about you send us the address?"

"It would be my pleasure. I'll text you just as soon as we

hang up." The sheriff paused. "Don't forget to fill me in on what you find out."

"I'll do my best," Colum said in the nicest voice he could muster.

"I'm sure you will." Clay chuckled. "And remember, keep your eyes on the sky. I'd hate for the two of you to get abducted."

19

Sheriff Clay's text came through less than a minute after Colum hung up. Twenty minutes after that, they arrived at a home several miles outside of town owned by a man named Jackson Rooke.

The property sat on a multi-acre spread. They passed a horse barn and paddocks on their way to a well-maintained single-story ranch house with a wide porch on the front.

Rooke must have seen them coming, because he was waiting at the door before they even arrived.

"You must be the FBI agents that Sheriff Clay told me about."

"That would be us," Colum said, flashing his fake ID as he approached the open front door.

"Gotta say I wasn't expecting to be taken so seriously. I guess the old TV show was right. The FBI really does have agents that investigate strange crap."

"I'd hardly compare us to that," Colum said, even as he smiled inwardly at the reference. "We're investigating a spate of unusual occurrences in town, and your experience might be relevant."

"Don't see how. It was just a bunch of lights in the sky."

"How about you walk us through it," Shelby said. "Show us where the incident took place."

"Sure." Rooke reached around the door and grabbed a coat. He put it on and stepped outside, closing the door behind him. "It was the horses that got my attention at first. They got all spooked about something and started whinnying. Figured a coyote must be sniffing around the barn, so I grabbed my gun and went over there."

"But it wasn't a coyote."

"No." Rooke led them across to the barn they had passed on the way to the house. "I checked the barn inside and out, but there was no sign of any predators. That's when I saw it. A circle of lights in the sky hovering over the horse paddock. Sent a shiver up my spine, I'll tell you."

"What were the lights doing?" Shelby asked.

"Nothing at first. They were just hanging in the air. It wasn't a plane or a helicopter. I know that much. It was eerie, seeing them suspended in the air like that and making no sound. I thought maybe it might be one large craft with lights around the rim. You know, like you see UFOs portrayed on the television. But then the lights started to spin and peeled off into a straight line even though there was still no sound of an engine or anything else."

Colum had his phone out was recording everything that Rooke said. "Where did they go?"

"Over yonder." Rooke pointed toward the trees at the edge of his land. "I watched until they disappeared, then checked on the horses again. They had calmed down and were back to their usual selves. I don't know how they knew the lights were there, but that was what spooked them. I'm sure of it."

Colum exchanged a look with Shelby. "That's the direction of Witch's Hollow." He turned his attention back to Rooke. "What time was this?"

Rooke shrugged. "Just before nine in the evening. I checked my watch to see how long I'd been out there." He looked sheepish. "Wanted to make sure I didn't have any of that... What do you call it? Lost time."

"You were worried about being abducted."

"Wouldn't you be?" Rooke rubbed his hands on his pants. "I know it sounds nuts, but I really couldn't think what the hell that thing could be except a UFO, or a bunch of them. That's why I called the Sheriff, not that he took me very seriously. Didn't think he was going to do anything about it at all until he called me back this morning and said the pair of you were on your way over here."

"I assume you hadn't lost any time," Colum said.

"No. I didn't hang around out here after that thing had flown off and the horses calmed down. Never been so happy to get back inside and lock my door. Barely slept a wink last night." Rooke sniffed. "Thankfully, the lights didn't return, and I didn't see any little green men."

"Did you take a photo of the lights?" Shelby asked, hopefully.

Rooke said nothing for a moment, then shook his head. "Probably should've been the first thing I did, huh? Then I would have had proof of what I saw. But I didn't even think about it in the moment. I was more concerned with the horses and my own welfare. Did anyone else report lights in the sky last night?"

"Not as far as we know." Colum gazed out across the

paddocks. "It must get pretty dark out here at night, being so remote. You ever seen anything strange in the sky before?"

"Nothing like that. Hope I don't see it again."

"I'm sure." Colum waited to see if Shelby had any more questions, then cleared his throat. I think we are about done here, Mister Rooke. Thank you for your time."

"Really? You aren't going to do any testing or look for more evidence of what I saw?"

"I'm not sure what testing we could do that would relate to lights in the sky," Shelby said.

Colum took a business card from his pocket. On one side was the FBI crest. On the other side was the name Special Agent Dale Winters and a phone number that connected to a burner phone provided by CUSP. "If you witness more strange occurrences, if the lights come back, I want you to call me immediately."

Rooke took the card and tucked it into his coat pocket. "Right. Of course. I'll do that. You can count on me."

"I'm sure we can." Colum turned the recorder app on his phone off and slipped the device back into his pocket. He let Rooke lead them back toward the ranch house and their car.

After they climbed in and were out of Rooke's earshot, Shelby turned to Colum. "You think he really saw a UFO?"

"I think he saw something. And the white light he described sounds a lot like what we saw on that cell phone video from Witch's Hollow."

"So aliens are responsible for what's going on here?"

Colum started the car and pulled away from the ranch house. "I'm not sure about that, but my gut is telling me those lights are connected to this, and my gut isn't often wrong."

20

COLUM AND SHELBY returned to the hotel and spent most of the afternoon sitting in front of their laptops, researching the history of the area, including Witch's Hollow. It turned out that most of the tales surrounding the old ruin in the woods were just that. There appeared to be no historical evidence to suggest that a woman named Abigail Fenton had ever lived in the area, let alone practiced witchcraft.

"It's not surprising," Colum said at one point, rubbing his tired eyes. "If the citizens of Blatchford ever burned a witch at the stake, it would have been all the way back in the late 1600s. Record-keeping was sketchy back then."

"Or Abigail Fenton might never have existed," Shelby said.

"That's also a possibility." Colum went back to his work. Having drawn a blank with the legend of Abigail Fenton, he moved on to another equally dubious line of inquiry. Unidentified flying objects. On this front, the record was just as sparse. There were no reports of UFO sightings to be found anywhere online. It appeared that if aliens existed, they had no interest in visiting Blatchford, Pennsylvania. At least until Jackson Rooke witnessed a circle of lights hovering over his horse paddock.

By seven o'clock that evening, having discovered no new information or leads, Colum decided to pack it in for the day. He closed his laptop and pushed it aside, then waited for Shelby, who was sitting on the other side of the table, to do the same. "Want to go find some food?"

"Sure. I could eat." Shelby pushed her chair back and stood up. "Give me half an hour to shower and change?"

"Take as long as you need." Colum waited for Shelby to step through the adjoining door into her own room and closed it behind her before standing up.

He crossed to the bed and sat with his back propped up against the pillows, then reached for the TV remote. A moment later, he heard running water. He clicked the TV on and settled back, closing his eyes, and using it as background noise.

A moment later, the connecting door burst open and slammed back on its hinges.

Colum sat up with a jolt.

Shelby appeared, gun in hand. She was still mostly dressed. She had discarded her sweater, and let her hair down so it flowed over her shoulders.

She ran to the window. "What are you doing laying down like that?"

"Waiting for you," Colum replied. "More to the point, what are you doing running around with that gun?"

"They might be out there." Shelby turned to Colum. She looked wild. Her eyes were wide, pupils dilated.

"You okay?" Colum stood up and approached her. "Did you pop a pill or something back there? You look strung out."

"No. You think I'm some kind of druggie?"

"I didn't say that." Colum nodded toward the gun. "Why don't you lower that and tell me what's going on."

"I told you. They might be out there." Shelby went to the window and used the barrel of the gun to part the closed curtains enough to peek out into the parking lot. "I don't see anyone, but that doesn't mean they aren't hiding."

"Who?" Colum was baffled. "You think someone is coming for us?"

"Don't you?" Shelby looked at Colum as if he were missing something obvious. She ran a hand through her hair, her eyes darting around the room. "They might even have this place bugged. It's not safe. We should leave."

"Okay. Timeout." Colum stepped toward Shelby and steered her away from the window. "There's no one out there and this room isn't bugged. What's gotten into you?"

Shelby slipped from his grasp. "The bathroom. We need to check your bathroom and make sure the room is clear."

"Shelby." Colum snapped his partner's name in an attempt to break through the sudden and obvious paranoia that gripped her. "There's no one else here but us. Put the gun down and we'll talk."

Shelby whirled around to face him. Instead of putting the gun down, she raised it in a two-handed grip, aiming directly at Colum's chest. "You're with them, aren't you?"

"Whoa. Easy there." Colum held his hands up, palms out. "I'm not your enemy. Please, lower the gun."

"You'd like that, I'm sure. You're just trying to buy time until they get here."

"I have no idea what you're talking about."

"Don't lie to me." Shelby's finger tensed on the trigger.

Colum held his breath. His heart pounded against his rib

cage. One tiny flex of Shelby's finger would send a bullet straight through him. His own gun was on the other side of the bed lying on the nightstand. Even if he could somehow leap sideways before Shelby got off a shot and make a dive for it, she would have no trouble putting a second bullet in him before he got there.

Shelby was backing up toward the door now with the gun still aimed at him. She reached the connecting door and locked it then went to the window again, never lowering the gun. She cast a quick glance outside, then turned back to Colum. "When did they turn you? Tell me or I'll put a bullet in your shoulder."

"I don't know what you mean." Colum swallowed, expecting her to shoot at any moment. "Who do you think I work for?"

"Don't play games with me."

"I'm not playing games and I'm not working for anyone except CUSP, just like you."

"Wrong answer. If you were on my side, you'd be more concerned." Shelby's voice trembled. "It's because I'm getting too close to what's going on here, isn't it?"

"Sure. Let's go with that." Colum decided to play along. It was his best chance of not getting shot, at least in the short term. "Tell you what. Lower the gun and you can ask me anything. What do you say?"

"Nice try. I'm not falling for—" Shelby paused midsentence. She blinked a couple of times, shook her head as if trying to fight off a mind fog. The anger fell away from her face. She looked down at the gun in disbelief, then up to Colum. "What just happened?"

"You tell me." Colum stepped sideways away from the line of fire.

"Sorry." Shelby lowered the gun and placed it on the table. She stood in silence for several seconds.

"You okay now?" Colum asked, his thudding heart finally slowing.

Shelby nodded slowly. Concern flashed across her face. "I think whatever has been happening to the residents of this town just happened to me."

21

At eight o'clock that night, Cheryl Potter was on her way to Bailey's Wine Bar on the south side of town for her usual Saturday evening tipple with the two friends from her school days, thirty years before, that still lived in Blatchford. She was on foot—the wine bar being a short fifteen-minute walk from her house—and making her way down Main Street when she saw someone else she recognized. Jayne Gibson, who, if not exactly a friend, at least fell into the casual acquaintance category. At least, she would have up until last month.

Jayne had been Cheryl's hairdresser for the last ten years and although she wasn't the most gifted of stylists, she usually managed to do a competent job for a dollar or two above what Cheryl felt was fair. But really, what was the alternative? Cutz and Curlz, Jayne's salon, was the only game in town. Or at least, it had been until four weeks ago when a shiny new business had opened up in the vacant unit that had once housed a dubiously planned business that sold nothing but gingerbread cookies. Now there were two hairdressers in town. And

Fantasy Cuts was not only cheaper than Jayne's until now unchallenged establishment, but the owner could spell.

There wasn't enough business in Blatchford for two hair salons, and Mindy Bartlett—recently transplanted from New York City and with an attitude to match—had swiftly gone on the offensive to crush Jayne's business under her heel with cheaper prices, better service, and the added incentive that every customer got a glass of wine when they entered. That was too good an offer for Cheryl to pass up, which was why she had switched allegiances within a week of the new salon opening.

She hadn't seen or spoken to Jayne in the weeks since, but quickly gauged her mood by the torrent of frustrated social media posts that lamented the sudden lack of business. Her old hairstylist was less than happy. Which was why Cheryl slowed, not wanting to come face-to-face with the woman and get pulled into the uncomfortable conversation that she was sure would ensue.

Cheryl turned to cross the road, hoping to slip past unnoticed, but then she stopped. Jayne wasn't paying any attention to her. In fact, Jayne was making a beeline straight for the new hair salon and what she was carrying sent a chill down Cheryl's spine. A brick in one hand, and a red plastic gasoline container in the other. Not the kind of thing you would expect to see someone carrying down Main Street on a quiet Saturday night.

Cheryl was caught in a moment of indecision. Jayne was clearly about to do something dreadful—and out of character. Complaining on social media was one thing, but vandalism was quite another. No, not vandalism. Arson. Because why else would Jayne be carrying that gas can?

Cheryl knew she should intervene, but that would mean putting herself in between her old hairstylist and the object of her wrath. She wasn't sure that was a wise idea, given the look on Jayne's face. But then she thought about Mindy Bartlett, who was not only cheaper than Jayne, but more friendly. Did she deserve to lose her business simply because she had the gall to compete with Cutz and Curlz?

The answer was obvious.

But if she was going to do something, it would have to be fast. Jayne had come to a stop several feet away from the salon. She drew her arm back and threw the brick.

The front window of Fantasy Cuts shattered.

Jayne walked closer, her feet crunching on broken glass. She lifted the gas can, splashing the liquid in through the broken window.

It was now or never.

Cheryl rushed forward as Jayne discarded the empty red container, reached into her pocket for a box of matches.

"No. Stop."

Jayne faltered, a match gripped between thumb and forefinger. She turned to look at Cheryl. "Well, if it isn't one of the traitors."

"What are you talking about?" Cheryl was breathless. She stopped short of the broken glass. "I'm not a traitor. I just changed hairstylists. That's all. We weren't even that friendly."

"You're my client, not hers." Jayne's face was red. A vein throbbed near the corner of her eye. "I've barely had ten bookings this week. I have to pay the bills."

"Then maybe you should try lowering your prices or giving people some reason to come back to you. Torching the competition isn't the answer. Why don't you put the match down and step away."

"Why don't you mind your own business." Jayne struck the match against the side of the box. It flared into an orange flame.

"Stop." Cheryl could see what was about to happen. She raced forward, tried to knock the burning match from Jayne's hand.

She was too late.

With a flick of her wrist, Jayne sent the burning match tumbling through the air toward the shattered window.

Cheryl held her breath as the flame shrank against the breeze and almost went out. The match disappeared inside the building even as the flame struggled to stay lit.

A second ticked by. Then another.

Cheryl relaxed. It was going to be okay.

At least until it wasn't.

A whoosh broke the silence, swiftly accompanied by a bright orange flash. A blast of heat belched through the window opening. Tongues of hungry flame devoured the building's interior like a hungry beast.

Jayne dropped the box of matches. She turned to Cheryl; face twisted into a demonic mask of glee. "Guess I'm the only salon in town again now."

"Jayne, what have you done?" Cheryl backed away from the raging inferno.

"I did what all good business owners do. Took care of the competition." She grinned. "See you on Tuesday at ten a.m. for your usual appointment?"

Cheryl didn't respond.

"Okey-dokey, then." Jayne rubbed her hands together.

Then she turned and strode away down the street as if nothing had happened.

Cheryl snapped out of her daze. She reached for her phone to call 911. But then she stopped, her attention drawn by another strange spectacle. A police cruiser stopped in the middle of the street. The driver's door was open. But the sheriff's deputy was ignoring the raging inferno consuming Fantasy Cuts. Instead, he was approaching a car parked across the street in a loading zone. He drew his gun, stood legs apart, and fired at close range into the vehicle.

"I'm—freaking—sick—of—people—parking—where—they—shouldn't." With each word, the deputy pulled the trigger again.

A tire blew out. The windshield shattered into thousands of beads. A curl of smoke rose from the engine compartment. Or maybe it was steam from the radiator.

The deputy holstered his gun and turned back toward the cruiser, climbed in, and continued down the street with his flashing bar lights silently painting the buildings on each side of the street in strobing tones of red and blue.

Cheryl watched him go, mouth agape, even as a shirtless man ran past, fleeing down the road as if trying to catch the cruiser. And behind him, doing her best to keep up, a woman brandishing a shovel and screaming at the top of her lungs.

22

"I COULD HAVE SHOT YOU." Shelby looked aghast. "I was right there, about to pull the trigger."

"Then I guess it's lucky for both of us that you didn't." Colum went to the table and picked up Shelby's gun. He placed it next to his own just in case Shelby had a relapse and decided to go for round two. After that, he walked over to the window and looked out. He half expected to see the black sedan sitting in the parking lot, but it wasn't. There was no obvious sign of whatever had affected Shelby. Colum turned back toward her. "How much do you remember?"

"All of it. One minute I was turning the shower on, and then I was overcome by this overwhelming paranoia and fear of betrayal."

"You said they were coming for us. Who were you talking about?"

"I don't know. Whoever is behind the strange events in this town. But that wasn't the root of it. It was like my insecurities were suddenly ramped up to insane levels. Whatever this thing is, it's setting off people's emotions and deep-seated fears. Like taking all the stuff we keep bottled up and pulling the cork out."

"So what are you keeping in your bottle?" Colum asked. "Because from where I'm standing, you were dealing with some major trauma."

Shelby sighed. "It's the reason I left the FBI." She crossed to the bed and sat down.

"Go on?"

"Several years ago, I was working a joint drug operation with a temporary partner assigned to me by the DEA. We went to see an informant about a shipment that was supposed to be coming in through the Port of Miami. The informant double-crossed us, and we ended up in the middle of an ambush. The DEA agent—his name was Peter Jasper—ended up dead. He had a wife and six-year-old kid. I blamed myself because the informant was mine. I'd used him before and trusted the guy."

"You couldn't have known."

"Easy for you to say."

"Is that when you came to work for CUSP?"

Shelby nodded. "After leaving the FBI, I locked all the emotions away and tried not to let them affect me. CUSP came calling and offered me a job, but I wasn't ready to get back into it. I told them no. They were very persistent, so in the end I took the job. I've been trying to put what happened at the FBI behind me ever since." Shelby winced. "I can feel a headache coming on."

Colum crossed to his bag, sitting on a luggage rack next to the TV stand. He rummaged around and came out with a bottle of painkillers. "Here, take a couple of these."

He opened the mini fridge and grabbed a bottle of water, which he also offered to her.

"Thanks." Shelby swallowed two pills and washed them down.

"What made CUSP want to recruit you?"

"I crossed their path on a case I was working up in Boston a couple of years before I quit the Bureau. Of course, at the time I didn't know it."

"What kind of case?"

"The latest in a string of homicides spread over six states. The victims had their throats cut, which on its own wouldn't have been enough to make us think there was a serial killer on the loose, given that we couldn't find any discernible pattern in the killings. Usually, a killer like that will stick to a certain type. In this case, each victim had the impression of what looked like a medallion of some sort left in the blood beneath their wound. The killer had pressed it against their skin. We never did find the killer."

Colum was silent for a moment. For the second time that day, he thought about Abraham Turner. He wondered if Shelby knew she had been chasing a vampire back then.

As if reading his mind, she answered the question. "After joining CUSP, I asked about that case, but they were tightlipped. I never did find out what the hell sort of monster I was chasing. But given what I know now, I'm sure it wasn't human."

Colum said nothing. It wasn't his place.

Shelby nodded toward the nightstand. "You can give me the gun back now. I promise not to shoot you with it."

"Guess I've got to trust you again sometime." Colum headed toward the nightstand, but before he got there, his phone rang. It was Sheriff Clay.

23

JACKSON ROOKE WAS in the barn feeding the horses when they started acting up for the second time in as many days. Spirit, a Quarter Horse with a light brown coat and white patch on her forehead, was the first to whinny. She stomped her hooves and tossed her head back. Soon the other horses joined in, filling the barn with their nervous cries. Rooke was ready this time. He dropped the feed bucket and raced to the back of the building, snatching up the rifle he'd stashed near the heavy double doors when he entered.

The chill night air whipped his face as he stepped out of the heated barn into the brisk November night and made his way around the side of the building toward the horse paddock.

And there they were, drifting soundlessly in the sky above the field. Ten white lights moving from east to west in a line. He couldn't tell how high they were or how big, but he knew one thing. They weren't meant to be there. Worse than that, they were upsetting his horses, and Rooke didn't like it when something distressed his animals.

He backed up a few steps without taking his eyes off the sky. and craned his neck up to look up into the inky black sky while slipping the phone from his pocket with his free hand. He hadn't taken any video of the objects the last time the lights showed up and didn't intend to make that mistake again.

The closest of them was almost directly overhead now. It was moving in a straight line with no visible means of propulsion. Rooke raised the phone and started recording, then tracked the object as it slid overhead. He panned to the left, capturing the rest of the loose formation, then stopped recording and put his phone away.

The closest of the lights was over the barn now. It slowed and came to a stop, hanging in the air as if suspended on an invisible string. The light pulsed and grew brighter. Its companions spun into a loose circle that swiftly tightened.

The racket from the barn grew louder. A cacophony of whinnying mixed with desperate snorts. Rooke didn't know if the horses could sense the threat floating above them, or if the UFOs—because what else could they be—were doing something to agitate the animals.

Either way, he couldn't let it continue.

Rooke raised the rifle and stared down the barrel, nailing one of the objects in his sights. He aimed slightly high, figuring that the main bulk of whatever the hell he was looking at must be above the light.

His finger curled on the trigger.

He fired a single shot.

If the bullet hit anything, there was no reaction.

Rooke took aim at the next light, aiming lower this time. But before he could pull the trigger, the lights rotated clockwise, gathering speed, and peeled off on their original course, forming into a line once again.

Rooke tracked the lead object and fired, anticipating its position and aiming slightly ahead of it to account for the forward motion.

This time, something happened. The light wobbled in the sky and lost forward momentum. The object immediately behind swerved to avoid a collision. Then, one by one, the lights circled around their wounded comrade and sped off toward the trees, faster than before.

Rooke chambered another round and lifted the rifle again, but the lights were zipping away fast and clearly out of range. All except the one he'd already hit. That object was limping along at a third of its previous speed and weaving an erratic path toward the woods.

It was easy prey.

Rooke aimed again and fired. Whatever he struck caused the light to tumble end over end in the sky before blinking out. But in that last second, right before the light was extinguished, he caught a glimpse of the object. A black circular mass that quickly dropped from the sky and vanished.

Rooke lowered the rifle.

The other objects were gone now. Vanished, as if they had never been there. But somewhere out in the woods, felled by a pair of shots from his rifle, lay the proof of what he'd seen.

Rooke hurried back to the barn and checked on the horses. They were calm now, and obviously hungry. He grabbed the feed bucket and went back and forth, making sure that each horse had its fill. Then he left the barn and hurried back to the ranch where he put on a thicker coat and grabbed a hefty flashlight before stepping back outside and striding toward the woods and the spot where the mysterious object had spiraled to earth.

24

THE FIRST THING Colum and Shelby noticed when they arrived in Blatchford was the burning building on Main Street. Two fire trucks were tackling the blaze, the firefighters aiming jets of water into the destroyed building and trying their best to stop the inferno from spreading to neighboring stores.

The second thing they noticed was the police cruiser on the opposite side of the road, parked near another vehicle that looked like someone had used it for target practice. Crime scene tape surrounded both cars.

Sheriff Clay was standing near the cruiser, observing the scene in front of him with his hands pushed into his pockets and a defeated look on his face.

Upon Colum and Shelby's approach, he pulled his attention away from the burning building. "Guess you were right. This isn't just a bunch of weird coincidences."

"Never thought it was." Colum nodded toward the police cruiser surrounded by crime scene tape. "What's the deal here?"

"One of my deputies decided he'd had enough with people parking illegally."

"So he shot the car up?" Shelby asked. "Wouldn't a parking ticket have been easier?"

"I would have thought so." Sheriff Clay sounded weary. "It's not every day you have to arrest one of your own for criminal damage." He rubbed his forehead. "What a mess."

"What did the officer have to say for himself?"

"Not much. Claims he was overcome by a sudden irrational anger." Clay looked toward the burning building. "Instead of bothering to take care of the situation across the street, he decided to vent on that car with his gun. Said that within minutes the anger vanished, and he was back to his old self. Had no explanation for what had possessed him except to say that he was fed up with people parking illegally on Main Street."

"Possessed might be the operative word." Colum nodded toward the building. "I bet you got a similar story from whoever was responsible for that."

"Jayne Gibson. Local hairdresser who decided to put the competition out of business. Literally. And yeah, she pretty much said the same thing. Driven by an urge that was too strong to resist."

Shelby cleared her throat. "Both your deputy and the hairdresser acted on things that were bothering them, albeit with excessive violence."

"Just like Maria Brock who murdered her cheating husband, and Megan Schultz who got fed up with her boyfriend doting on his car."

"And me becoming paranoid in the hotel room," Shelby said.

"Huh?" Sheriff Clay looked sideways at her.

DEADLY TRUTH

"Long story, which I'm not going into right now."

"Are these the only two incidents?" asked Colum.

Clay shook his head. "We have a woman who chased her boyfriend down the street with a shovel because she was fed up with him refusing to do yard work. Hardly the kind of thing you want to end up on attempted murder charges for. Oh, and a couple who smashed up the bathroom in their apartment because the landlord hadn't fixed a leaky tap quick enough. There might be more incidents we don't know about. I'm praying we don't have any more situations like Maria Brock on our hands that we haven't discovered yet." Clay sighed. "I don't suppose you have an answer for me on all of this."

"Wish we did." Colum watched the firefighters. They had all but doused the flames now, but the hairdressing salon would not be opening again anytime soon. The building was reduced to a smoking charred shell. The businesses on either side hadn't fared too well, either.

"This is going to keep happening, isn't it?" Sheriff Clay sounded despondent.

"It's a fair bet." Colum glanced upward toward the night sky. "This might sound like a strange question, but did anyone report seeing lights hovering overhead?"

"What kind of lights?"

"The kind that look like unidentified flying objects," Shelby replied.

"Hell. You bought into Jackson Rooke's crazy story?"

"He was adamant about what he saw."

Clay snorted. "Aliens don't exist. Or at least, if they do, they aren't zipping around our skies doing stuff like this."

"Can you be sure of that?" Colum asked.

"I'm not even going to dignify such a crazy theory by

discussing it." Sheriff Clay folded his arms and glared at Colum. "Find me some answers that make sense, and then we'll talk. In the meantime, I'm a deputy down, so unless you have any constructive suggestions on how to deal with all this, you'll have to excuse me."

"Hey, you called us out here."

"Because I thought you might actually be of some use."

"Sorry to disappoint you, Sheriff."

"Forget about it." Clay stomped off toward a gaggle of deputies, waving his arms and shouting at them.

Colum's phone rang.

Jackson Rooke was on the other end of the line.

Colum listened to what he had to say, then hung up and turned to Shelby. "You ready for things to get even weirder?"

"I have a feeling they're about to, ready or not. What's going on?"

Colum glanced toward the sheriff, who was several feet away now and paying them no attention. "That was the guy we met yesterday. The one with the horses. He says the UFOs came back tonight."

"Really?"

"Yep. And apparently, he shot one down." Colum was already making for their car. "Let's go."

25

Rooke was standing on his front porch when Colum and Shelby pulled up. He wasted no time in racing down the steps to meet them at the car.

"You got here fast. That's good. You don't have anything to do with those helicopters that have been flying over, do you?"

"No." Colum shook his head. "What helicopters?"

"A pair of Black Hawks. They were circling the woods near where the UFO went down. Had searchlights and everything." He grinned. "But they won't find it. I already went into the woods and dragged the dang thing back here."

"You hauled the UFO all the way back here on your own?" Shelby looked skeptical.

"Sure did. With the help of my 4x4. Luckily, it crash landed right off an old logging trail so I could get up in there with the truck. Figured it wouldn't be long before the people operating those helicopters expanded their search and came calling. After all, they probably know I shot it. That's why I called you guys. You may be with the government and all, but you strike me as decent enough people. I'm not sure the same can be said for whoever is behind what's been going on and I'd rather not end up disappearing, if you catch my drift."

"Maybe you should have refrained from shooting at whatever was flying over your property?" Shelby said.

"Yeah. Hindsight is twenty-twenty." Rooke shrugged. "Too late now. Want to see it?"

"What do you think?" Colum looked around. "Where is it now?"

"Still in the back of the truck. Didn't have time to unload it before those helicopters started buzzing around." Rooke led them toward the horse barn and drew the large double doors back. Sitting inside, in the wide aisle between the stalls, was a black heavy-duty truck with oversized tires and a row of spotlights mounted on a bar above the front bumper. He went to the back of the truck and dropped the tailgate. "I was going to hide it in an empty horse stall and then figure out what to do."

"Probably not the wisest course of action," Colum said, peering into the truck bed. The object Rooke had retrieved from the woods was covered by a blue tarp. He reached in and grabbed a corner, then pulled it off.

What sat in front of them was not a UFO, although it bore a passing resemblance to one. It was around four feet wide and disc-shaped, with four rotor blades on stalks that extended from the sides of the craft. A dome-shaped cover beneath which Colum could see a mass of electronic components protected the body. A square box sat beneath the craft. What looked like a single light from a distance was actually four small spotlights arranged one on each side of the box and pointing downward. Four retractable legs sat folded underneath the craft, presumably in their flight position. A bullet hole was visible on the upper dome, the edges curled outward, signifying that the bullet had entered from beneath and exited through the dome, which was dented with impact damage along one side. Somewhere along the way, the bullet must have taken out a vital component which brought the vehicle down.

Colum drew in a long breath. "You're right. That isn't a UFO. It's a drone."

"That's what I thought." Rooke laid a hand on the contraption. "Except it's bigger than any domestic drone I've ever seen and packed with electronics I can't identify."

"One of these must have been in the sky above Witch's Hollow." Shelby leaned in to get a closer look. "I bet there was one above our hotel earlier this evening, too."

"Not to mention Main Street." An image of the burning building flashed through Colum's mind. Was this vehicle, or others like it, responsible for all that carnage? If so, then why?

"Someone's up to no good," Rooke said. Voicing what both Colum and Shelby were thinking. "I bet it's some deep state black op testing out their latest toys. Just another example of our government using us like guinea pigs."

"Wouldn't be the first time," Colum said.

Rooke furrowed his brow. "Blatchford seems like a strange place to do it, though."

"I bet that's what the good folk of San Francisco thought when the CIA started experimenting on them with LSD during the fifties."

"Project MKUltra," Shelby said. "They used federal inmates as test subjects, as well. And it wasn't just the CIA. Military researchers got in on the action, too."

"The military." Colum was examining the drone. "That's my best guess for whoever is behind this thing."

"And there's more of them," Shelby said. She turned to Rooke. "How many did you see flying over your property?"

"Six of them last night. I didn't bother counting when they came back tonight. But I did get a video before I shot at them." Rooke took out his phone and clicked around before handing it to them with the video screen ready to play.

Shelby and Colum watched it, then handed the phone back to Rooke. Shelby looked sideways at Colum. "You think they work in tandem, or individually?"

"Impossible to know. But judging by the number of incidents and distance between them, I bet they can work on their own. It affected you at the hotel around the same time someone was trying to torch a hair salon on Main Street."

"Good point." Shelby eyed the drone. "How do you want to proceed?"

"We have to get this thing somewhere safe," Colum said, avoiding any reference to CUSP. "It's too big to fit in our car. We need to call in a retrieval team."

"That could take hours and the drone won't be safe here."

"We don't have a choice. With any luck, whoever owns this thing will take a while to track it down."

Rooke's phone chirped. He looked down at it. "I wouldn't be so sure. I have a motion activated surveillance camera down near the road. Three vehicles just turned on to the property. Black SUVs. They're coming up the driveway now, and they don't look friendly."

"That only gives us a couple of minutes," Colum said. He was already pulling the tarp back over the drone. "Ideas?"

"They catch us here with this thing and we'll be in a heap of trouble," Shelby said. "Depending on who they are, we might even end up vanishing without a trace. We need to leave right now."

Rooke pulled a set of keys from his pocket. "Take the truck. Go."

"What about you?" Shelby asked. "You can't stay here. It's not safe."

"I'm not leaving the horses. Besides, they can't do much to me if there's no drone here."

"I wouldn't be so sure about that," Colum said. But he took the keys anyway and headed toward the cab, then shouted over his shoulder to Shelby. "Get in."

Shelby raced around to the passenger side. "Wait. How are we going to get out of here with those SUVs coming up the driveway?"

"No idea." Colum slammed his door and started the truck. "But it's better than sitting here and waiting."

26

"THERE'S a dirt trail out back of the property," Rooke said. "It leads through the woods. Follow it until you reach a split in the trail then go left. Beyond that, there's a covered bridge. Two miles after the bridge you'll intersect Route Eighty. You should be okay if you go that way. Most of the trail cuts across my land and no one really knows about it."

"Thanks." Colum pulled the truck forward.

Rooke raced in front of it and stuck his head out through the barn doors. "All clear so far. You're good to go."

Colum gave him a thumbs up and exited the barn, turning left and following the driveway toward the house. He picked up the trail that ran around the side of the building and back through a wide pasture toward the woods circling the property. The shine of headlamps from beyond the horse barn reflected back at him when he looked in his rearview mirror.

"They're coming," Shelby said, twisting in her seat and peering back through the truck's rear window.

"I can see that." Colum pressed down on the accelerator, urging the truck to go faster.

A gap between the trees opened up ahead of them. This must be the trail Rooke had told them about.

When he risked another glance behind him, Colum saw that one of the SUVs had stopped in front of the barn. The other two were still coming, following the truck even though he was running dark. No lights.

"Hold on." Colum sped up more, feeling the truck's bulky tires bite on the soft earth beneath them. The 4x4 would have little trouble navigating the uneven terrain. He wondered if the pursuing vehicles were similarly equipped. He hoped they weren't but knew better than to assume. "This is going to get bumpy."

Shelby reached up and grabbed a handle above the passenger door. "If they figure out where we're going, they might call ahead and block the trail."

"We'll worry about that when it happens." Colum gripped the steering wheel tight, fighting against the juddering vibrations relayed through the steering column.

They reached the trees and the woodland trail. Not a moment too soon. A searchlight pierced the sky. The steady throb of heavy rotor blades was audible over the roar of the truck's engine.

Colum craned his neck to look up through the windshield and saw a sleek shape flitting through the sky. This was no drone. "Black Hawk. It's looking for us."

The searchlight stabbed down through the trees, splashing the ground behind them in a brilliant white haze. Beyond this, the two SUVs were still coming.

"I think they've seen us," Shelby said, breathless. She drew her gun and rested it on her lap.

"Tree canopy gets thicker ahead." Colum turned the wheel to avoid a yawning pothole. Despite his best efforts, the back left wheel dropped down into it with a jarring thud.

Then they were into the thickest part of the tree cover. The trail veered to the right. The searchlight didn't follow. Instead, it kept going straight.

"We lost them," Shelby said.

"For now." The whoop of rotor blades grew faint, then louder again as the helicopter flew back and forth, looking for its prey.

Behind them, the SUVs kept coming, although they were falling behind thanks to the rugged terrain. Colum could see the dual pinpricks of their headlights piercing the night. Worried he might drive them into a tree, Colum flicked his own headlights on, aware that the red glow of his taillights would give the SUVs a point of reference.

"How are we going to lose them?" Shelby asked, craning her neck to look behind her.

"The split in the trail is up ahead." Colum pushed the accelerator all the way to the floor. They were flying along at a dangerous lick now. The trees whizzed by mere feet from them on each side. One wrong move and they would wreck the truck.

Reaching the split, Colum threw the steering wheel hard to the left.

The truck careened into the bend.

The back wheels lost traction for a second and Colum thought he might lose control, but then the truck righted itself and shot forward.

Realizing he had no choice, Colum turned the truck's lights off again and hunched forward over the steering wheel, doing his best to stay on the dark trail.

Shelby was still looking through the rear window.

The SUVs were at the split in the trail now.

They slowed, clearly unsure which way the truck had gone.

Then they split up, each going in a different direction.

"Down to one SUV, but it's coming fast," Shelby said, turning forward again.

"Don't worry. I have an idea." The shape was looming out of the darkness. The covered bridge Rooke had told them about. Colum steered underneath it and slammed the brakes on, then flung the driver's side door open and hopped out, reaching for his gun at the same time. He glanced back toward Shelby, who was already exiting the vehicle on the passenger side. "Follow my lead."

Kneeling at the back of the truck, Colum aimed back down the trail even as the SUV's headlights drew closer. He sensed Shelby at his side. "Fire low to the ground and take out their tires." His finger tensed on the trigger. "Wait for it."

The SUV was close now. The dazzle of its headlights was blinding.

Colum squinted against the glare. "Now."

He squeezed the trigger even as Shelby did the same. The twin booms were deafening.

The SUV swerved and for a moment Colum thought it would go into a tree, but then the driver regained control and brought it back onto the trail.

"Again," Colum shouted, realizing that if they failed this time, they would be caught. Or worse, the SUV would plow into them, and then crash into the back of the stationary truck.

Colum aimed to a point below the right headlight and fired. Shelby took the left.

Another two booms.

The SUV swerved again but this time it didn't recover. Instead, it bumped down off the trail and disappeared into the darkness beside the covered bridge. There was a resounding thud, followed by a loud splash. The SUV was lying on its side in a fast-running stream that coursed under the bridge. Its front was crumpled. There was no movement from within the vehicle. The wreck hadn't been violent enough to kill the occupants, which meant they were probably just stunned.

Colum jumped to his feet. "Come on, let's get out of here before anyone else shows up."

He jumped in the truck's cab and waited for Shelby to climb in, then flicked the headlights on and pressed down on the accelerator. The truck lurched forward even as a second set of headlights appeared in the distance behind them. But it didn't matter, because they were tearing along now toward Route Eighty and would be gone by the time the occupants of the second SUV, which must have doubled back, reached their fallen companions.

That only left the helicopter, which appeared to have moved off to search further afield. With any luck, they would exit the woods unseen and make their escape. The only question was, where would they go?

Shelby must have been thinking the same thing. "You realize we can't go back to the hotel?"

"I know." Colum risked a glance skyward, but there was still no sign of the Black Hawk. "But we can't stay here either. We need a place to hide and examine that drone. Figure out what we are dealing with."

"Then we only have one choice," Shelby said. She took her phone out. "I'm calling Sheriff Clay."

27

SHELBY FINISHED TALKING to Sheriff Clay as they arrived at Route Eighty.

"He said to come straight to his house. He's finished up on Main Street and he will meet us there." Shelby put the phone away. "Told us to be careful. There were some federal types who wouldn't identify which agency they were with sniffing around after we left."

"I bet they were looking for us," Colum said. He sat at the intersection, engine idling, eyes lifted to the dark night sky. "We appear to be a thorn in someone's side."

"Especially since we snagged what looks like a covert ops drone." Shelby leaned forward and looked up. "You think that helicopter is gone?"

"No. It's around somewhere. But I don't think we have much choice but to move. If we stay here, we're sitting ducks." Colum inched forward and turned onto the road.

Shelby had already gotten directions to the sheriff's house, which turned out to be several miles away on the outskirts of town.

As they drove, Colum stared out into the darkness, looking for any sign of the Black Hawk. At first he saw nothing, but then the steady thrum of rotor blades filled the air. The helicopter appeared over the tree line to their left, far too close, and dropped until it was hovering twenty feet off the ground directly in their path. A pair of stubby wings flared on each side of the upper fuselage and below them, a weapon Colum recognized all too well from his time in the military.

His blood ran cold.

"Hellfire air-to-ground missiles." He slammed on the brakes and cursed, throwing the truck into reverse, and backing up. "Laser-guided and lethal up to five miles."

"That sounds bad." Shelby stared through the windshield.

"It's worse than bad. We can't avoid them, and unless this truck can break the sound barrier, we can't outrun them. They fire one of those things at us and we'll get about half a second to say goodbye before it's over."

The helicopter was still sitting there blocking their path, but it made no move to fire on them.

"What are they waiting for?" Shelby asked.

"Good question." Colum steered the truck in reverse as fast as he dared. He didn't want to take his eyes off the helicopter, even though he knew it would make no difference to their situation. "Maybe they don't want to destroy their drone and are waiting for their colleagues in the SUVs to catch up with us."

"I don't think so." Shelby pointed. "Look."

The helicopter was on the move again. It rose into the sky, hovered a moment more, nose pointed down toward them, and then banked and raced off to the east. The road behind them was empty. There was no sign of the remaining black SUV.

Colum brought the truck to a halt. "That was weird."

"Hey. Not complaining." The relief in Shelby's voice was clear. "Better than being vaporized by a Hellfire."

"Agreed." Colum put the truck back into forward gear and started off down the road again, following the directions from Shelby's phone. "I still don't like it, though."

28

THEY ARRIVED at Sheriff Clay's abode, a large Victorian-style house that sat on at least an acre, a little after ten. He was already waiting and motioned them around the back of the house to a barn that stood with its doors open.

Colum pulled inside and came to a stop. By the time he climbed from the truck, Clay had flung the doors closed and turned the lights on.

The barn was large, with a second-floor hayloft above, although there was no hay. Shovels and rakes and all manner of other garden tools hung on one wall. A riding mower was parked in the back of the barn. On the other side was a workbench that Ran the length of the wall. Colum recognized a lathe, ban saw, and a heavy-duty miter saw. A pegboard affixed to the wall held hand tools.

Clay approached the truck. "Did you run into any trouble?"

"Not unless you count a heavily armed Black Hawk helicopter and a bunch of goons driving SUVs."

"One of those SUVs didn't fare too well," Shelby said.

"What about the drone?"

"It's in the bed." Colum went to the back of the truck and dropped the tailgate, then pulled the tarp off. "Honestly, I thought that Black Hawk was going to incinerate us to destroy this."

"I'm still not sure why they didn't." Shelby stared at the drone. "We were in their sights."

Clay was studying the drone with wide eyes. "This is what's been causing all the trouble in my town." He leaned close. "There's a bullet hole in it."

"Courtesy of Jackson Rooke." Colum jumped up into the bed and kneeled next to the drone, examining it up close.

"I hope he's okay," said Shelby.

"Me too." Colum stood and went to the other side of the drone. He motioned to Sheriff Clay. "Help me lift this thing down."

Together, the two men wrestled the drone out of the truck bed and set it on the soft earth of the barn. Now that it was unloaded, they could get a better look. Colum could see the path of the bullet through the machine. It had taken out a bunch of wiring and pierced a printed circuit board. One of the four rotor blade arms was bent, damage that had probably happened when it plowed into the ground.

He inspected the equipment hanging from the undercarriage but had no clue what any of it did.

Colum straightened up. "We need to get someone with more experience on this, and fast, if we're going to figure out what this drone is capable of."

"Maybe." Colum took out his phone and scrolled through the contacts, then placed a FaceTime call.

A moment later, a familiar face filled the screen. Rory McCormick. Fellow CUSP operative, archeologist, and electronics geek extraordinaire. He looked bleary-eyed and tired. "Colum O'Shea. What the hell are you doing calling me at this time of night?"

"It's not that late," Colum said.

"It is in France." Rory yawned. "I'm on a job."

"Sorry." Colum did some mental arithmetic and figured out that it was three-fifteen in the morning there. "I need your help and it can't wait."

"All right. Give me a moment." The phone screen went blank. A minute later, Rory came back on. This time, he looked more alert. "What have you got?"

"This." Colum flipped the phone camera so that instead of showing his face, it showed the drone sitting on the barn floor.

"Whoa. That looks like a serious piece of tech. What did you do, raid a DARPA lab?"

"Not quite." DARPA stood for Defense Advanced Research Projects Agency. They reported to the Department of Defense and were tasked with developing new technologies for the military. Colum had briefly wondered if that agency was responsible for the incidents in Blatchford, but quickly dismissed it. They were a bunch of geeky scientists, not shady black ops people. Whoever was behind this was much more dangerous. "A local rancher shot it down after six of them flew over his property. We think they are tied to a series of strange events, but we don't know how."

"Okay. Fill me in, but be warned, I'm an archaeologist. I can't guarantee to be of any help."

"You're so much more than an archaeologist," Colum said. "You dabble in all sorts of stuff and probably have more knowledge locked up in that brain of yours than most quantum physicists. That's what makes you such a valuable asset."

"Enough with the flattery. Get on with it."

"Fair enough." Colum filled him in on everything that had happened, starting from the original incidents in town all the way up to their encounter with the Black Hawk on the road outside of Jackson Rooke's property.

Rory listened in silence. After Colum finished, he sat lost in thought.

"Well?"

"Show me the drone again. Turn it upside down so I can see the good stuff."

Colum complied with Sheriff Clay's help. They rested the drone on its back before the Irishman panned his phone camera across the electronics sitting beneath the strange vehicle.

At one point, Rory told him to stop and zoom in on a particular component. A flat circular disk with tiny slits in the surface secured to a gimbal, allowing it to move swivel and tilt independently of the drone's position.

"There. That's your problem," said Rory, his voice tinged with excitement. "I'm sure of it."

"What does it do?" Colum asked.

"Not easy to explain." Rory sounded excited. "But I think it's an acoustic weapon of some sort. It looks a little like the LRADs developed by the military, only more compact and advanced."

"LRAD?" Clay asked.

"Long range acoustic device."

"You mean like sound waves?" Shelby asked.

"Something like that." Rory was talking fast now. "We're probably talking high-frequency focused ultrasound or some similar technology. There's been some research into sound waves above the capacity of human hearing and their effects on the brain, which can help alleviate mood swings and depression, among other things. But at different frequencies, it can also cause negative emotions like paranoia and sudden anger. Now, of course, all of this is speculation, and the sound waves would have to be delivered with pinpoint accuracy."

"Maybe that's why they're using six drones instead of one," Colum said. "To produce more of a blanket effect."

"It could also mean that each drone is targeting a specific person or small group of people," Rory said.

"There's still one thing I don't understand," Shelby said. "The bats that swarmed out at Witch's Hollow."

"That's an easy one," Rory said. "Bats navigate using ultrasound. Maybe the drone interfered with that ability. It might also have drove them into a panic, causing them to swarm."

"Sounds as plausible as anything," Colum said.

"And it's also more proof of what this thing can do," Rory replied. "If we assume the drone is testing some sort of high-frequency sound weapon, then my next question is, what do you plan to do with it?"

Colum switched the camera, so Rory was looking at him instead of the drone. "I haven't really thought that far ahead. We were too busy trying to get away from helicopters and SUVs full of goons to figure out much of a plan beyond going to ground."

"Weird thing is that they gave up so easily," Shelby said.

"They let you go?" Rory sounded concerned.

Colum nodded. "One minute we were staring down the missile launchers of a Black Hawk, the next it was letting us go on our way."

"I can't think of a reason why they would do that," Shelby said.

Rory was silent for a moment. "I can. What if they're able to track the drone, even in its damaged state?"

"I hadn't thought of that," Colum admitted. "But it would make sense. Rather than taking us out in a public way, they could wait until we stop moving and get rid of us quietly."

"So why haven't they done that already?" Shelby asked. "We've been in this barn for a while."

"Maybe they want to approach the situation carefully, since they're dealing with a pair of FBI agents and the local sheriff." Colum didn't know if their FBI cover would hold up to scrutiny by an entity with the resources this one appeared to have, or maybe they were just regrouping, but either way, there wasn't much time. They needed to come up with a plan, and quickly.

Shelby must've been thinking the same thing. "I hate to say it, but maybe we should ditch the drone before we end up in a situation from which we can't escape."

"Or maybe you use it to your advantage," Rory said. "My guess is that the drone has some sort of homing capability. Once its mission is over, it will probably return autonomously to wherever it was launched from."

"I'm not sure I like the idea of delivering the drone right back into the hands of whoever was operating it," said Colum.

"Normally I would agree. But think about it. The drone could lead you right to them."

"How?" Colum asked. "We'd never be able to keep it in our line of sight long enough to follow the thing."

"You won't need to. I bet the drone has some sort of transponder allowing it to be tracked by whoever is operating it. If we can lock onto that signal, we can do the same thing in reverse and track it back to their base."

"How?"

"Easy. All I need to do is figure out the frequency that drone is transmitting on, and I can use . . ." Rory paused. "Well, let's just say that our employer has access to a certain satellite with the capabilities we need."

"You mean like a military satellite?" Shelby asked.

"No. More like CIA, although they would never admit to owning it."

"Oh."

"I probably don't want to know about this," Sheriff Clay said. "You people aren't with the FBI, are you?"

Colum met the sheriff's gaze. "I'd prefer not to answer that." He addressed Rory again. "Will it work?"

"Sure. I'll be able to track the drone and send you its location in real time."

"Even from France?"

"Absolutely. Wonders of the digital age." Rory yawned. "But you'll owe me big for this. I won't be going back to bed any time soon."

"Consider us in your debt," Colum grinned. "There's only one problem. The drone is damaged."

Now Rory grinned. "Then let's fix it."

29

THE DRONE SAT on the dirt path outside Sheriff Clay's barn. It was midnight. Colum had worked on the drone for ninety minutes, with Rory guiding him through each step of the repairs from a continent away. Sheriff Clay and Shelby had assisted where necessary, retrieving tools, keeping the drone steady, and holding a flashlight for Colum to see what he was doing inside the complicated craft.

Once the damage from the bullet's passage had been patched up, they walked it outside and waited to see if the drone would reboot.

"You don't think this thing will self-destruct, do you?" Sheriff Clay asked, observing the machine from a distance with folded arms.

"This is not an episode of some science fiction show," Colum replied. But even so, he backed up a few paces away from the drone.

It didn't self-destruct.

After what felt like an eternity, but was probably only two minutes, during which the machine made a series of high-pitched whines, spun its four independent rotors at varying speeds, and flashed its lights, the drone lifted from the ground and hovered at an altitude of ten feet while its landing gear—four spindly legs—retracted and folded into place under the fuselage. Then it rose higher into the air and moved off to the north.

Colum watched it go with a mixture of apprehension and satisfaction. It had taken longer than expected to repair the drone and he had spent that time nervously anticipating the arrival of a Black Hawk helicopter or maybe even a couple of the SUVs that had showed up at Jackson Rooke's horse ranch. But they had been left in peace, much to Colum's surprise. Now, the drone was doing exactly as Rory had predicted and returning to its point of origin.

He looked down at the phone and Rory. "Please tell me you're tracking that thing."

"I'm watching its progress as we speak," Rory said. "It's heading toward Blatchford on a course that will take it east of the town. If you're going to follow it, now would be a good time to start. I'll relay the directions to you in real time."

"Already on it." Colum was heading back toward the barn and Rooke's truck. He hopped in and reversed the vehicle out onto the trail, then waited for Shelby to climb in. When Sheriff Clay went to follow, Colum held his hand up. "I think it's best if we handle it from here."

"Not a chance. This is my town, and I'm sworn to protect it." Sheriff Clay shook his head. "You leave me behind and there will be an APB out on this truck before you've made it half a mile down the road. Your choice."

"Dammit." Colum's fingers tightened on the steering wheel. He sat a moment with the engine idling, then grimaced. "Fine. Get in. But a warning. Anything you see or hear from this point on is classified. You so much as utter a word of our activities tonight and you'll find yourself out of a job quicker than you can count to ten."

"Or worse," Shelby muttered.

"Okay. I get it. My lips are sealed." Clay heaved himself up into the cab and waited for Shelby to push over on the bench seat. He clicked his seatbelt and turned toward Colum. "Well, what are you waiting for?"

"Nothing, I guess." Colum handed the phone to Shelby and started back around the Sheriff's house toward the road. As he went, he conversed with Rory. "All right. I'm all yours. Tell me where to go."

"Head toward town, then back out onto Route Eighty." Rory's face filled the cell phone screen. His eyes were cast downward, toward what Colum surmised was a laptop out of view. "The drone is moving fast now. It's already beyond the horse ranch."

"Thank goodness Jackson Rooke didn't try to shoot it down again," said Shelby.

"Maybe he's learned his lesson on taking pot shots at unidentified flying objects," Colum replied.

"Or maybe he's being held by those goons who showed up at his house."

"No time to check on him." Colum was already zipping down the road back in the direction they had come from. He kept his eyes to the sky for any sign of a Black Hawk helicopter intent upon intercepting them. Thankfully, the sky was clear. "He's on his own, at least for now."

"I can send a couple of deputies over there," Sheriff Clay said, reaching for his phone.

"Great. Do it. But tell them to be careful." Colum pushed

the truck faster. "We don't know who these people are or what they're capable of."

"The drone has stopped," Rory said from the phone handset. "Looks like it landed."

"Where?"

"Middle of nowhere. Deep in the woods off of Route Eighty. I don't even see a road leading to it on any maps."

"Just send us the coordinates. We'll take it from there."

"Already on it."

Colum waited for Shelby to confirm that they had received the drone's last known location. He told her to enter the coordinates into the truck's GPS system. Just like Rory said, the location was a couple of miles into the woods beyond Route Eighty, with no visible means of access.

"There must be a road," he said, glancing at the screen. "Those SUVs would need a way in and out."

"Question is, why isn't it on the map?" Shelby asked.

"Covert bases rarely are." Colum was flying along at thirty over the speed limit now. "Sure wish we could get an imaging satellite over that location."

Rory's voice drifted from the cell phone handset. "Not going to happen on such short notice."

"Shame. I would love to know what we are walking into."

"Guys," Rory said. "The transponder on the drone just turned off. It's gone silent."

"You think they realized we're coming and are trying to hide their location?" Colum asked.

"Who knows. I'm not picking up any other transponders from that location, either. You said there were six drones in total, so maybe they just shut them all down."

"Maybe." Colum glanced toward the phone. "You should get some sleep. We've taken up enough of your time."

"You sure?" Rory asked. "I hate to leave you in the middle of this."

"Unless you can get us that imaging satellite, there's not much more you can do right now."

"Roger that." Rory hesitated. "Just be safe, I'll set up an alert on that drone. If it moves again, we'll know."

"Good job. Stay close to the phone. Will call if we need anything else."

"Sure thing." The line went dead on Rory's end.

Colum was still watching the GPS. "Keep your eyes peeled. We're almost at the closest point to the drone's location. There has to be a road around here somewhere, even if it's only a dirt trail."

"What about that?" Shelby was leaning forward and staring through the windshield. Up ahead was a turnoff blocked by a pair of chain link gates. It was the only opening visible along that section of highway for at least a mile in each direction.

"That must be what we are looking for." Colum slowed as he approached the turnoff, then came to a stop in front of the gates, his headlights illuminating a narrow dirt trail that wound through the woods into impenetrable darkness. A sign on the gates read, 'Private Property—Keep Out'. Another, smaller sign notified them that the area was under twenty-four-hour surveillance, and trespassers would be prosecuted. A small camera mounted on a pole barely visible near the trees reinforced that message. Colum eyed the camera warily. "There goes the element of surprise."

"I'll get the gates." Sheriff Clay pushed his door open and jumped from the truck. He raced around the front. The gates were not locked. He swung them open. First one, then the other.

"This is a little too quiet, don't you think?" Shelby said, scanning the darkness ahead of them.

"Like the calm before the storm." Colum waited for Sheriff Clay to climb back into the cab, then he lifted his foot from the brake and inched forward off the road past the gates. He was grateful for the Glock pistol sitting snug in his shoulder holster. "Here goes nothing."

30

THEY FOLLOWED the dirt trail for a couple hundred feet until it turned to the right. Here, out of sight from the road, the trail widened and turned to asphalt.

"Someone wanted to make sure this place wouldn't be given a passing glance," Colum said as they bumped up onto the pavement. He looked skyward to see a thick canopy of tree branches arching over the road and blocking the night sky. "Even from above, you'd never see this road. Even with satellite imagery, Rory wouldn't find a route to where the drone landed."

"I'm the sheriff in these parts and I didn't know this was here," Clay said. "I must have driven Route Eighty a thousand times and never noticed it. Of course, it might not have been here for long. Those gates looked pretty new."

"A temporary facility, maybe?" Shelby asked.

"We'll find out soon enough." Colum followed the road as it wound a serpentine path through thick woodland and finally opened up into a cleared area with felled trees cut into logs and stacked near the perimeter, almost like a protective wall of wood. Except that within this outer ring was a ten foot high chain-link fence topped with razor wire.

Another set of gates on the road ahead stood open as if inviting them in. Beyond this were several prefabricated buildings and three areas that were clearly landing pads. There was no sign of the drone, but a single Black Hawk helicopter rested on the furthest pad.

"That isn't the one that harassed us," Shelby said. "No wings or weapons attachments."

"This place looks dangerous," Sheriff Clay said, leaning forward and peering through the windshield. "We'd better be careful."

"It also looks abandoned," Colum said. "I don't see any personnel or activity."

"Maybe everyone's asleep," said Shelby. "It is late."

"While leaving the gates open and not bothering to post a guard?" Colum shook his head. "Something's not right. I can feel it in my gut."

"All the more reason to proceed with caution."

"Always do." Colum slowed the truck as they approached the open gates and came to a stop. "Thoughts?"

"Could be a trap." Shelby's hand went to the gun sitting in a holster against her ribs.

"A pretty obvious one, if it is," Clay said. "I mean, c'mon. Leaving the gates open, the compound exposed and vulnerable? Surely they would be smarter than that."

"Unless that's what they want us to think," Colum said.

"If this was a trap, wouldn't they have sprung it already?" Shelby craned her neck and peered through the truck's rear window. "It wouldn't take much to block our retreat and go on the offensive."

DEADLY TRUTH

"True." Colum found it hard to believe that the people operating those drones would lay such a clumsy trap as to leave their facility exposed and an escape route wide open. He lifted his foot from the brake and let the truck roll forward. "I'm going in. It's the only way to find out what is going on here."

They passed through the gates and approached the closest building. The helicopter stood further away and to their right, it's rotor blades motionless. Colum couldn't tell if there was a pilot onboard.

He brought the truck to a halt again.

"What now?" Shelby asked.

"I think we're about to find out," Colum said, because there was someone else inside the compound, after all. A door opened in the building directly ahead of them and a solitary figure stepped out, then approached the truck. A man wearing all black, with broad shoulders and a muscular build. He stopped ten feet ahead of the truck and stood with his arms folded.

"I guess this is our welcoming committee." Colum resisted the urge to reach for his Glock. Instead, he reached for the door handle and pushed the driver's door open, then unclipped his seatbelt and climbed out.

"I was wondering how long it would take for you to show up," the man said as Colum approached him and stopped a few feet in front of the truck. "Thank you for returning our drone, by the way."

"You're welcome." Colum sensed movement to his right. Shelby and Sheriff Clay were both out of the truck. "Your helicopter could have fired on us out on the road earlier this evening. Why didn't it?"

"It would have been messy. Air to surface missiles fired

upon civilian vehicles on public roads tend to draw unwarranted attention. We prefer to remain in the shadows."

"And later, at the barn?" Colum asked. "I'm sure you tracked the drone."

"Just like you did when you followed it back here." The man smiled. "But again, the same answer. We originally hoped to reacquire the drone quietly at that horse ranch before you could get your hands on it, but it didn't play out that way. We arrived a bit too late."

"Speaking of Jackson Rooke," Colum said. "Your men had better not have hurt him."

"What do you think we are, savages? When we realized the drone was not there anymore, we left him in peace. Told him we were with the DEA and that the drones were being used by a cartel to smuggle narcotics. Warned him not to breathe a word of what had occurred there. I think we were quite reasonable, considering he shot down a very expensive piece of equipment."

"You're not with the DEA."

"Obviously."

"And that drone wasn't being used to smuggle drugs. It was fitted with a high-frequency sound weapon that affected the mental states of whoever you aimed it at."

"Very good. Worked pretty well, too, for a first field test."

"People are dead." Colum kept his voice level despite the anger rising inside him.

"That was unfortunate, but we gleaned a lot of information."

"Which makes it all okay?" Shelby took a step forward, reaching for her gun.

"I never said that." The man held up a hand. "I wouldn't do that if I were you. I wasn't foolish enough to remain here alone." He nodded toward the Black Hawk. "There's an assault team waiting inside that helicopter. If you open fire, so will they. None of you will make it out of this compound alive."

"I knew it." Sheriff Clay glanced around nervously. "This is a trap."

"Actually, it's nothing of the sort." The man smiled. "Our work is done here, and we've already moved on. All we needed was that final drone which you so kindly repaired."

"How did you know we wouldn't just keep it," Colum asked.

"Because I know who you work for and it's not the FBI. I've had dealings with Classified Universal Special Projects before and you're so predictable. I knew you wouldn't be able to resist tracking the drone back to its point of origin. I also knew you wouldn't find anything when you got here. Except for myself, of course, and I'll be on that helicopter just as soon as we finish this conversation. After that, feel free to tear this place apart. It won't do any good."

"You closed this place down then stayed behind just to wait for us?" Colum was skeptical.

"Of course. It wouldn't be any fun to just vanish into the night and leave you guessing. I want your boss to know that we're still around and only getting stronger. How is Adam Hunt, anyway?"

Colum said nothing.

"What about John Decker?"

Colum wasn't about to answer, but he had a question of his own. "Who are you, and what organization do you work for?"

"The organization I work for isn't important. But I would

like you to relay a message to Hunt. Tell him Thomas Barringer sends his regards."

"Barringer?" Colum scoured his memory to figure out why that name sounded familiar. Then he remembered. "You were involved in the German U-boat mess down on Habitat One."

"Ah. My reputation precedes me. I also broke out of your unofficial maximum-security prison and took a little trip down to the Amazon, where I bumped into my old friend, John Decker. Your boss is going to be most aggrieved that I slipped through his fingers yet again."

"What makes you think we're letting you go anywhere?" Colum started toward Barringer.

The Black Hawk's side door slid open. Four men in tactical gear stepped out and raised their weapons.

"That's far enough, I think. Unless you want me to send my message back to Adam Hunt via three body bags."

Colum stopped. He clenched his fists, fingernails digging into the palms of his hands.

"Now, if you'll excuse me, I have places to be." Barringer turned and strode toward the helicopter. He climbed in and waited for his men to do the same before turning in the doorway and looking back at Colum. "Feel free to look around after we're gone, but I wouldn't take too long. There are explosive charges in all the buildings. Once we're airborne and at a safe distance, they go boom."

Barringer retreated inside the helicopter.

The door slid closed.

The Black Hawk lifted from its pad and rose into the frigid night sky.

Colum briefly thought about whipping out his gun and putting some well-placed bullets through the helicopter's windshield, but the forward firing mini-guns mounted to the cabin windows were enough to convince him it would be a foolhardy endeavor. Instead, he watched as the helicopter rose higher in the air, then swooped over the facility in a tight bank and flew off toward the north.

"We should probably get out of here," Sheriff Clay said, turning back toward the truck. "If what that guy said was true, this place is about to be an inferno."

"Dammit." Colum desperately wanted to search the buildings but had no reason to believe that Thomas Barringer was lying.

They were on borrowed time.

He sprinted back to the truck with Shelby beside him and they jumped in. Then he slammed into gear and pulled a tight turn, racing back through the gates, and down the narrow access road as fast as he dared to drive.

And not a moment too soon.

A series of booms ricocheted through the woods even as the clearing behind them exploded in a mass of searing orange flames and thick, acrid smoke, that belched into the sky.

EPILOGUE

THREE DAYS LATER

AFTER MAKING sure everything was taken care of in Blatchford, which included swearing an unharmed Jackson Rooke to secrecy and coming up with a suitable cover story about the explosion in the woods with Sheriff Clay, Colum and Shelby had been recalled to CUSP's island HQ off the coast of Maine.

Now they sat in Adam Hunt's office while their boss read through the report they had submitted on the events that occurred in the small Pennsylvania town.

When he was finished, Hunt closed his laptop screen and observed them with narrowed eyes. "A drone mounted ultrasonic weapon that can alter the mindset of those it's used against and compel them to act out their deepest fears and hidden truths. It sounds like science fiction."

"But it's not." Colum glanced at Shelby. "We experienced the weapon firsthand."

"So I gather." Hunt leaned forward, resting his hands on

the desk and intertwining his fingers. "A device like that could cause havoc on the battlefield. Imagine aiming it at an enemy tank during the height of an engagement. The crew might let their fears overcome them and become incapacitated, or worse, turn the gun and fire on their own side."

"Which would be a strategic advantage in the hands of our own military," Colum said.

Hunt nodded.

Colum continued. "Or a severe liability if it fell into the hands of less friendly nations. Do we know anything about the group who were testing this device in Blatchford? Because I got the impression that they were not necessarily friendly."

Hunt sighed. "All we know is that they have deep pockets, are well organized, and appear to operate without impunity. For all I know, they're some Pentagon black ops unit, rogue."

Colum was silent for a moment. "Thomas Barringer."

"Yes." Hunt's face looked like thunder. "He's becoming a real thorn in our side."

"He appears to have a beef with both you and John Decker."

"John was responsible for foiling his plan on Habitat One and stopping him from escaping with a piece of valuable alien technology. I'm the one who put him in a maximum-security CUSP facility that he promptly escaped from—killing one of our own men in the process, I might add. Beyond that, I'm not sure what his agenda is other than to sow chaos."

Shelby had listened silently so far, but now she chimed in. "If Thomas Barringer and his organization are not working for a facet of our own government or military, then this weapon could very well end up in the wrong hands."

"I would say it already has," Hunt said. "Regardless of Barringer's affiliations, he's reckless and self-serving. I fear he also has an agenda bigger than we previously realized."

"Then let me go after him," Colum said. "After what he did in Blatchford, I'd be more than happy to put him back behind bars."

"I second that," Shelby said.

"Not so fast. We already have people looking for him. People who know what they are doing in that arena."

"The Ghost Team," Colum said, referring to CUSP's quasi-military unit used for everything from mop up to covert operations. Colum had worked with some of them before and knew them to be capable operatives. If they couldn't find Barringer, no one could.

"Yes. Although I don't hold out much hope of finding him." Hunt leaned back in his chair. "But no matter. He'll surface again soon enough. Like you said, he holds a grudge against us, for whatever reason."

"What's next, then?" Shelby asked. "A nice, easy assignment on a beach in the Caribbean?"

"I can't promise you that." Hunt grinned. "But you have earned yourselves a few days' rest and relaxation."

"I won't say no to that," Colum said. "Maybe I'll head down to Boston and check out some of those legendary Irish bars." He glanced at Shelby. "Want to come with?"

She shrugged. "Sure. Why not?"

"Fantastic. I'll show you a good time you'll never forget."

"Don't get your hopes up. Strictly platonic."

Colum feigned a hurt expression. "I'll have you know I'm a gentleman. I would never think it was anything but platonic."

"Yeah. You just keep telling yourself that." Shelby laughed.

"And since you're such a gentleman, the first round is on you. Maybe the second one, too."

"You've got it, *Special Agent North*."

Hunt shook his head. "All right. That's all I can take. Get out of here and enjoy your down time. I don't want to see either of you back here until Monday."

"Awesome." Shelby pushed her chair back and stood. "Come along, *Dale*. We've got some Boston pubs to visit."

"Works for me," Colum said, following her toward the door. "But just so you know, if you call me Dale one more time, the deal is off. You can buy your own drinks."

The next book in the CUSP Files series
Devil's Forest - coming soon

In the meantime, try another book by Anthony M. Strong
The Remnants of Yesterday
Available in paperback, e-book, and Kindle Unlimited

THE NEXT BOOK IN THE CUSP FILES SERIES

Devil's Forest

When a group of campers in the Maine wilderness are attacked by a large, bipedal creature they claim to be a Bigfoot, John Decker is sent to investigate, and what he finds is stranger than he ever would have believed, and just as deadly...

Coming soon

To be notified when Devil's Forest is available for pre-order join my mailing list at https://anthonymstrong.com/list

ABOUT THE AUTHOR

Anthony M. Strong is a British-born writer living and working in the United States. He is the author of the popular John Decker series of supernatural adventure thrillers.

Anthony has worked as a graphic designer, newspaper writer, artist, and actor. When he was a young boy, he dreamed of becoming an Egyptologist and spent hours reading about pyramids and tombs. Until he discovered dinosaurs and decided to be a paleontologist instead. Neither career panned out, but he was left with a fascination for monsters and archaeology that serve him well in the John Decker books.

Anthony has traveled extensively across Europe and the United States, and weaves his love of travel into his novels, setting them both close to home and in far-off places.

Anthony currently resides most of the year on Florida's Space Coast where he can watch rockets launch from his balcony, and part of the year on an island in Maine, with his wife Sonya, and two furry bosses, Izzie and Hayden.

Connect with Anthony, find out about new releases, and get free books at **www.anthonymstrong.com**

Made in the USA
Middletown, DE
03 October 2023